I0671482

FROM
STRIPPER
TO
SAINT

FROM STRIPPER TO SAINT

A NOVEL

DAVINA E. BROWN

EMPOWERING
Books Publishing House

FROM STRIPPER TO SAINT

Copyright © 2021 by Davina E. Brown
Cover Design and Illustration by Adam Lee Harden

All rights reserved. In accordance with the U.S. Copyright Act of 1976, the scanning, uploading, and electronic sharing of any part of this book without the permission of the author or publisher constitute unlawful piracy and theft of the author's intellectual property. If you would like to use material from the book (other than for review purposes), prior written permission must be obtained by contacting the author at DavinaEBrown@gmail.com. Thank you for your support of the author's rights.

This is a work of fiction. All of the characters, names, incidents, organizations, and dialogue in this novel are either the products of the author's imagination or are used fictitiously.

Empowering Books Publishing House (EBPH)
Bartlett, Tennessee 38134
empoweringbooksph@gmail.com

Please check out our other books online at empoweringbooksph.com

ISBN-13: 978-0-9971-0289-5 (sc)
ISBN-13: 978-1-9563-1601-8 (eb)

Library of Congress Control Number: 2021914224

This novel is dedicated to Serenity. Thank you for making me the woman I am today. It's because of you that God saved me from myself.

Thank you to my family and friends who supported me over the last year and a half.

I did it! My first novel is done!

With love,
Davina

PROLOGUE

"It's a boy!" someone yelled in the packed delivery room. The lighting was dim, and a dull atmosphere greeted me into a large room with foggy windows on pale green walls. I could smell weird fragrances. Something spicy and musky hung in the air.

"No, no," the doctor corrected. "It's a baby girl."

And loud cheers erupted from the background. But the two people closest to me appeared the happiest.

"Look, baby, we did it." The woman pulled me closer to her chest.

"You did well, love. She's perfect!" The man put an arm around her and smiled down at me. I felt warm and safe. Gazing into my big, brown, almond eyes, my mother whispered, "I love you."

The room went quiet, and I was strangely aware of everyone staring at me, the newest addition to their family.

A few minutes later, I began glancing around the room, blinking and winking at everyone and everything. *Wow, this place is so different. I can stretch my legs and make unique noises. My mother is beautiful, and people are staring at me. What is this place?*

My mother handed me over to my dad. He smiled and made a funny face. "Booweecoo! Daddy's girl," he shrieked in joy. I laughed and giggled.

Soon, all family members were taking turns to hold me. Some kissed my forehead and some breathed in my baby scent while others clicked their fingers to make a snapping sound. I couldn't stop giggling. I loved the attention.

Finally, my dad passed me to my grandmother. There was a sudden surge of positivity inside me when she took me into her arms. I could feel a fuzzy warmth in my tiny heart as she held me close. She was crying, but her eyes lit up brightly when I tugged at her finger. Her lips opened and closed as if she were talking in an inaudible language, and then she blessed me with a kiss.

After that day, I learned quickly about this new place that was my new home. My parents cared for me and cheered me on when I made discoveries – even the simplest ones, like wriggling my legs and swinging my hands.

"She's so cute and pretty," they would say.

I liked my new home. It was different from the earlier tight, watery place. There was clean air, and I could breathe with my nose and mouth alike. I could move as much as I wanted to. The hard yet fuzzy surface felt nice underneath my body.

I kept on growing – crawling, hobbling, walking, falling, walking again and again. From "Da-da" to "Daddy," "Ma-ma" to "Mommy," I began to walk and talk. Observing more, learning more, wanting more, I began to grow into myself, Naomi.

***

A light breeze wafted the smell of fried chicken and collards greens. I could barely wait to eat. But as we pulled into the wide driveway of my grandma's yellow and white house, I heard them yelling. Getting out of the red 1990 Cadillac Deville lined in gold, I ran over to the gate and peeked through the door. It was Mom and Dad arguing. Again. And this time it was physical.

"Marcus, I'm done! I can't do this anymore. Naomi is growing, and she needs her dad to be home! Your gigging isn't supporting us like it should!" Mom was shouting at the top of her voice.

"Susan, I don't understand. I've gone on international gigs before, and it was all fine. What makes this one so different?" Dad reiterated.

"It's different because I will still need to work these two jobs, and your paycheck won't even cover Naomi's daycare. Plus, you know my mom doesn't have the strength to watch her all the time."

"But this is the gig we've been waiting on, baby! I'm performing with a legend. This is big for us, can't you see?"

"It's big for you. Not for us. You took a pay cut to go on this gig and didn't think about us and our needs. I'm done!"

I knelt beside the door and pushed it open.

Out flew my baby doll.

NO! I almost screamed but caught my voice. *Not my favorite doll.*

She was a "Baby So Real" doll. She could drink water from a bottle and eat all the mushy stuff I gave her. *Not her, not my doll.* As I stared at my doll that lay twisted on the floor, I cried out.

"Mommy, Daddy!" I was distraught. "What's going on?"

They froze. My mom looked at me tearfully and dropped my stuffed animal that she was holding. She ran across the room to the bathroom, closing the door. My dad eyed me anxiously for a moment before bending down and kissing my cheek.

Then he sighed and perked up with a smile. "Let's go get some ice cream, shall we?"

"Okay, Daddy," I replied, my face brightening up instantly, all thoughts driven out of my mind.

We hopped into his blue 1987 Oldsmobile Coupe and went to get some ice cream. When we got home, it was as if nothing had ever happened. The house was quiet, and my parents didn't say much to one another. Nevertheless, that night, I slept with my grandma.

Chapter One

"Red lights. Go!"

My dance coach yelled at the lighting supervisor, "Now add a beam of dazzling white light. Yes, right, she needs a dramatic entry." She winked at me before turning to another spot boy. "We need loud drumbeats. Let the sound expert know the exact frequencies I have shortlisted."

The spot boy nodded and rushed out of sight. I stared at her as she circled around, checking the lighting, costumes, and backstage arrangements. Then, with a sigh of relief, she turned to me.

"You're so little, Naomi," she said, watching me with her deep hazel eyes. I flinched, not sure if that had been a compliment. She smiled. "Yet you're the fiercest dancer I've ever seen."

I felt my cheeks go warm, and blood rushed to my limbs. I timidly returned her smile.

Seconds later, faint music filled the air, and my dance coach straightened, clearing her throat and escorting me towards the stage entry.

"Naomi," she called out loudly, "hold your head high and square your shoulders. Lead with your toe pointed and stretch that leg, girl. Now go and shine!"

I nodded and took a deep breath before leaping to one side of the stage. I turned and spun across to the left, ending with a split center stage. A remix beat of "Songbird" by Kenny G fused through the auditorium, and I let my body move, momentarily closing my eyes and forgetting the world.

It was my first solo performance, and the minute my toes grazed the floor, I found a natural rhythm between the two. I was born for this.

As I covered the stage with my gracious moves, nothing else mattered. It didn't bother me that I was only ten years old and vastly smaller in structure than the other girls. My body relaxed and swirled as the music flowed through my veins. I felt my light breath moistening the air, and I took a deep, happy inhale, a wide smile stretching over my lips. *I'm Naomi, the dancing princess. I own this stage.*

***

It was 1997, and my mom and I lived in a two-bedroom, blue and white lined luxury apartment in the desert suburbs of Las Vegas, Nevada. The only sound we could hear was the noise of fighter jets at Nellis Air Force Base. This was my home now.

My grandma had passed away a year before, and it took a toll on my mom. Having little choice and not knowing we'd be homeless, she sent me to live with my uncle in Modesto, California. Modesto was much closer to my birthplace and my dad. It turned out to be the ultimate vacation for me.

Living with my uncle, I was the Queen of the house.

"Naomi, please feel free to live however you want in this house, like it's your very own," Uncle boomed with a wonderful laugh. "Your bedtime is 8 o'clock, and I'll get you registered for school tomorrow."

I smiled at him. It was hard not to smile around him. My uncle was a petite, flamboyant man who loved nature and beautiful people. He was excited to have me living with him. I was his only niece and the only child on his side of the family. He and my mom were siblings. Uncle and his partner loved the idea of kids but could not have any due to their relationship. But most of all, Uncle had a resounding voice that appeared more like an eternal laugh.

"How does that sound? Or would you like a day off?" He smacked his lips together.

"Tomorrow is fine," I replied, grinning at him. "I don't want to get out of my regular school routine."

"Ah… what a good girl you are, Nomi," he said. "How about some warm milk?"

Nomi was my family's nickname for me. My uncle was the first to use it, and it stuck.

"Um… I have never had that before."

"Are you kidding me, girl?" He bounced up out of his chair with a fake raspy voice and began chuckling, unsurprisingly reminding me of my mom.

"Here is a glass of my special warm milk," he said, as he handed me a large glass of milk. "Now, Nomi, this is a miracle drink. It will help you forget all worries and grief. Sleep well, my dear."

I kept staring at the glass for a few minutes after he left the room before slowly taking a sip. It felt good. Then I put the glass to my lips and drank until it was empty. It worked. Just as Uncle had said, I could feel my homesickness and the grief of losing my grandma fade away.

This is a miracle drink! I wondered *why it couldn't save my grandma from someone or something everyone called "The Cancer."*

***

"You've got The Cancer, Ma!" my mom said for the hundredth time to my grandma. "You've got to tell those folks at your job!"

But no, like every other time, Grandma shook her head and refused to leave work. I recalled numerous arguments about her still wanting to work despite "The Cancer." She was a strong-headed woman and had refused to quit working because "The Cancer" was in her. She'd worked and worked up until her dying day.

"Grandma, please don't leave me," I told her when she was bedridden in the hospital. "I need you."

"I'm not going to leave you," she said. "Come, lie down with me."

Determined to be with my grandma, I overcame my shy self and jumped headfirst onto the bed but fell on the floor instead.

"Get up, my pumpkin," Grandma called softly. "Try again."

I got up and made another attempt. This time she grabbed my hand and pulled me close. The hospital smelled of old people, medicines, and alcohol, but lying next to Grandma, I could still smell her characteristic scent of roses lingering on her gown.

"Jesus loves me, this I know, for the Bible tells me so. Little ones to Him belong, hmm, hmm, hmm, but He is strong, hmm, hmm, hmm…." Her feeble voice hummed in my ears, and soon, we drifted off to sleep.

When I woke up, I was all alone in the hospital bed. Panic gripped my soul. I didn't know what had happened, but I had a weird feeling that something was terribly wrong.

"Mom," I called out, "where is Grandma?"

Hearing my voice, Mom came rushing inside the room. Her face was ashen with swollen eyes and tears washing down her cheeks. "Nomi..." she croaked.

"Mom," I gasped, watching her distraught expression. "Where's Grandma?"

"Oh, Nomi, my baby," she said amidst sobs, "your grandma has gone to heaven. You were both asleep, and she was holding you tight... She loves you, baby, and she is always going to be with you."

Her words didn't make sense to me, as I was still in the same hospital bed. The same one we'd fallen asleep in. Together. I didn't feel anything, nor did I know what'd just happened. That was my first encounter with death and "The Cancer."

***

"Nomi, Naaaoomiiiii!" Uncle's voice rang in my ears. "It's time to wake up for school. I don't want you to be late on your first dayyyyy!"

Rubbing my eyes and exhaling in a wide yawn, I jumped out of bed. My dreams were vague, and I couldn't remember much. Anyway, I was excited. New school, new friends, new everything! It would be a good distraction.

The new teacher, an old, short woman who had a calm voice and spoke eloquently, introduced me to my new class. The classroom was big. The windows seemed to erupt from the floor and touched the ceiling. And they widened across a whole wall. There were not many students, thus making the room appear even more spacious than it already was. The lingering scent of Elmer's glue and paint flushed the room's essence, giving it that familiar smell of my old classroom. After realizing I was the only girl that looked like me, I took a seat and prepared myself to start the first day of school.

"So?" Uncle raised his eyebrows while we walked back home. "How was your first day, Nomi?"

"Good, but it's different for sure. The kids and teachers are nice, but I noticed I'm the only Black girl in my class, and during recess, it was just me. Still the only one."

"I understand. It is different, but I am sure you'll get used to it, Nomi."

"I suppose," I answered, walking down the street holding my uncle's hand.

***

That year passed quickly, and my mom was finally on her feet. She was able to cope better and be there for me.

"Welcome home, baby," she said, running up to me and pulling me in for a tight embrace at the airport.

"Mom!" I yelled and hugged her back.

I felt happy to be with her and proud of myself for helping her overcome the grief.

"Thank you for being Mommy's big girl and going with your uncle."

"Of course, Mom," I replied. "Are you feeling better now?"

"Yes, Mommy is better now. I couldn't control the grief when your grandma passed away, but I'm better now," she said as we drove home.

Home sweet home, I thought, glancing out the window.

After returning home from Modesto, Mom felt it was best that I rejoined my old school. She wanted me to settle in as easily as possible. I was happy with this decision. Now I didn't have to worry about making new friends or being the "new kid." I was just Naomi who left and came back.

"Naomi, welcome back!" my friends and teachers would say. I was back and happy to be home!

***

When the song neared its end, I stood in the center of the stage and posed beneath the spotlight. The crowd burst into thunderous applause, and a familiar voice broke through all others.

"That's my baby!" Mom was yelling in joy while Dad stood beside her with watery eyes and a proud grin pasted on his face.

I rushed over to my parents after the show.

"So, what did y'all think?" I asked, suppressing a shy smile.

"That was awesome!" Mom almost shouted, drawing the attention of several people around us.

"Mom…" I shushed her, laughing.

"What?" Mom guffawed and raised her eyebrows. "Aren't I allowed to be a proud mother and boast about my little dancing sensation?"

"Of course, Susan," Dad chimed in with a smile. His brown eyes met my inquisitive ones, and I noticed they were still wet.

"Why were you crying, Daddy?" I asked, gazing up at him. "Didn't you like my performance?"

He crouched down on his knee, so his eyes were at my level. He paused for a moment, as though assessing something heavenly on my face, and then he said, "I cried because I was so happy, sweetheart. My emotions were too much to handle for a simple smile."

I looked at his face – dark brown eyes, dark brown hair cut low to his head, and dark, smooth skin with high cheekbones. Weary but peaceful.

"And about your performance," his lips cracked into a handsome smile, "that was the most beautiful thing ever."

I grinned and put my arms around his neck. He stroked my hair in a playful embrace.

"This was better than those piano lessons, for sure!" he said, and we pulled apart laughing harder.

"Dad, will you be staying the weekend?" I asked after a while.

"No, sweetheart, Daddy has to get back to work in California," he said. "I'll see you for spring break."

"Okay, see you then," I said. "Call me when you're home."

"Daddy loves you. Bye."

My parents had been divorced for a few years now, so it had somehow gotten easier to say goodbye to Dad without Mom having to drag me away from him.

CHAPTER TWO

"Sir, I need three tickets. I'm trying to get my girls into the concert," said Mesha's mom. My friend Mesha and I waited anxiously to see if we'd actually get in.

"I got extra tickets, ma'am, but I need $90 for each ticket," a man with a deep voice called out.

"I'll give you $75 a ticket, and I ain't giving you the money until we all get in past security."

"You a tough mama!" the man said, laughing.

"You're laughing? I'm serious, man. My girls gotta see this concert," she affirmed.

"Alright, alright, $75 a ticket, and I'll get the money once y'all walk through."

"Great! Girls, let's go!" she called out to us excitedly. She'd delivered on her promise of taking us to the Janet Jackson concert.

As the lights dimmed, the crowd began roaring. The stage was dark, and I was confused.

Where is Janet? I thought she'd be on stage once we got to our seats.

The stadium was packed with people, and it smelled of popcorn and liquor. I was so excited, there were butterflies in my stomach. I was unable to set my expectations. This was my first concert, and Mesha's mom had gotten us in. Spotlights began roaming the stage; the stadium began to rumble.

"Wooooooo! Janet!" I did what everyone in the stadium did. They screamed, I screamed; they chanted, I chanted. The model of a big book appeared on stage. It opened like a TV screen, and I'd never seen a TV screen this big. Lost in the TV, she appeared – Ms. Jackson, staring into the crowd, not moving.

Is she real? Is this real? Oh my goodness, I'm seeing fucking Janet Jackson! "Wooooooo!"

I'd seen her a million times on TV and imagined watching her live concert. Never could I muster the courage to tell Mom or Dad, though. I'd lost hope of ever having access to her before I became an adult. Yet here I was. Here she was.

She stood in the middle of the stage, wearing a black suit with a white shirt underneath.

No less than a Goddess.

With her zeal, confidence and allure, she owned the stage. And from that moment on, I wanted to be Janet Jackson! The crowd roared with her every move. I was stunned at first, and then I too began roaring with the crowd. The band queued the music, and "IF" began. I remembered watching this video on MTV and imitating her moves, including the hip roll. Her moves in the concert mirrored her moves from the video.

Head roll to the right. Head roll to the left. Jump and throw up your hands. Grab the guy by the neck, toss it back and forth. Get on top of him and squat down.

My body moved to the beat, and my eyes were glued to the stage. *Oh my goodness, I think I'm going to faint. I am really here, watching Janet!*

The concert was full of passion, colors, and awe! Suddenly, the lights went off. We understood it was the end and began pleading with Mesha's mom to let us stay out a bit longer. Somehow, she agreed with a sly smile. Mesha and I looked at one another and didn't question it. *We grown tonight,* I thought.

The lights flickered, the intermission was over, and the lights began to go dim again. My friend and I looked at one another with wide eyes and began to cheer. Mesha's mom just looked at us and laughed. "Y'all thought it was over, huh?"

We nodded and laughed. She continued, "We have a long and late evening, ladies. Enjoy it because this will be it for a while."

We giggled, knowing there would be more. Her mom was always taking us out.

Janet pulled a man on stage from the crowd. She made him sit on a chair in the center and tied his wrists. He was going crazy with passion and jubilance. He kept repeating, "I love you, oh my God, I love you!"

She didn't say a word. A sly, naughty smile displayed on her lips. Then she jumped on top of him and began dancing in his lap. He sat there in a trance. Janet was all over him, and the man was going crazy by this point. His eyes were glued to her body in a mesmerized stare.

I want to do that to someone one day! I thought.

Janet led the man off stage with her crew of dancers, and I wondered if they were going to do it now, but they returned and continued with the show. Janet Jackson's Velvet Rope Tour 1998 taught me how to hypnotize a man by looking at him and owning my walk and talk. That

Monday, going back to school, I felt superior to my peers because they hadn't seen Janet, nor did they know what I knew about *men and doing it.* That night, I was sure I'd discovered the meaning of sexy and sensuality, and also everything about sex.

CHAPTER THREE

My dad met Karen not too long after his divorce from my mom. She was a kind white woman with long golden hair that reminded me of Farrah from the old *Charlie's Angels*. Her eyes were deep blue as if they held the ocean in them. I didn't think much of her and respected her because of my dad. I was raised to respect my elders, so Karen was treated with respect.

She had a young daughter, Tessa, from a previous marriage. Tessa became the little sister I never had.

Summers were spent in Santa Cruz, California.

Santa Cruz was different than Las Vegas. Santa Cruz had waves while Las Vegas had deserts. Santa Cruz gave me freedom, while Las Vegas gave me babysitters and playtime in the front yard. Santa Cruz felt rich, and Las Vegas felt like a struggle. Santa Cruz was a vacation, and Las Vegas was home.

The sea breeze blew lightly in the air as Tessa called out, "Naomi! Let's go hike down to the beach."

"Okay, but we need to let your mom know before we go so she doesn't panic," I replied.

"You call her because she'll say no to me," Tessa said.

Karen had been married twice before. The birth of Tessa was the biracial seed of her second marriage. She had had two sons from her first marriage, but since they were adults, they were on their own, and little Tessa, youngest of three siblings, only saw her brothers on holidays.

Somehow, Tessa always felt that her mother favored me whenever I was around. I never saw it. I always thought it was Karen being nice, given that I only came to see them during occasional breaks.

I called her on the phone, and Tessa was right.

Karen said, "Yes, of course, you both can go, but make sure you only hike on the low tide rocks. I'll meet you girls in Capitola."

Capitola was the cool spot. The Beach Boardwalk was right there, and we loved it there. We went on rides and played games. I always considered Santa Cruz to be the safe spot in my life, but soon, it turned dreadful.

***

Tessa and I were sitting in her room behind the bed, away from the loud shouting and crying.

"Tessa, it's going to be okay. I'll protect you. They are just arguing; it'll pass." I tried to comfort her.

"They always argue, Nomi. I wish I could go home with you to Las Vegas," Tessa cried.

"Aww, don't worry, don't worry." I rocked Tessa back and forth.

She continued to shake and whimper. After a while, when she was finally about to calm down, we heard plates and other tableware being thrown on the floor, shattering in an instant.

Karen's voice rang with spite. "What the fuck! You just gonna leave like all the others! Fuck you, Marcus!"

Tessa began shivering, and we crouched low, folded together, hiding in the corner behind the bed. *This lady is crazy, and I can't wait to tell my mom about this!* I held Tessa tight and prayed, *Lord, please protect my daddy and us.*

The fight continued for over an hour, and then everything grew silent. I was aware of the aftermath – having faced similar situations in my parents' marriage – but I knew my mom to be an awesome person. And until then, I'd pictured Karen to be kind and loving. But here it was. The truth.

"Girls, get up! We're going to get ice cream," Dad said, bursting into the room and hurrying us out of the front door. Ice cream was Dad's way of making everything all right. The ice cream melted our fear of Karen away.

"Dad, why do you put up with Karen?" I asked. "She is mean to you."

Dad's eyebrows fell, and he looked away. He didn't seem angry, though, because he laughed seconds later. Perhaps he was embarrassed at my straightforwardness. Seeing his reaction, I didn't expect him to answer, but he caught his breath and sighed, "It's okay. She had a dream that I was going to leave her. She's been through a lot, and I understand how hard her life has been. Above all, I love her."

"But Dad, she said some horrible things to you. It must have hurt a lot, I know. Plus, you and Mom have always taught me to be kind and respectful towards people." I looked up at him with a curious twinkle in my eyes.

"Yes, baby, we do, but sometimes people who love one another argue, and that's normal. We can't break up over something as little as a dream. Sometimes our experiences in love can lead to bad memories. And although it's very natural, we have to stretch through those memories to move forward and love people again. Karen's last marriage ended in a disaster, and she's got some uncomfortable and painful memories. She's still healing from that. But don't worry at all. Daddy will be okay."

"I guess, but how can you still love her when she says hurtful things, like the F-word, to you?"

"I know she doesn't mean it. We'll chat later about our argument, and everything will be fine."

He breathed in sharply and sighed again. "You'll understand when you get older, and love in your life moves beyond Mommy and Daddy."

I pondered over his statement. It irked me how most of my curiosity discussions led to this ultimate conclusion where I was asked to wait until I was older. Wasn't I already old enough to comfort Tessa and bravely hide behind the bed when something happened?

While I was lost in my thoughts, Dad watched me carefully. "Naomi," he said, "I love her, and I hope you're able to look past this argument and be a good girl for Karen."

I nodded, although my mind was still racing with retorts. *Love her! Yuck. I know that wasn't love; that was crazy!*

That day, I realized how people loved differently, and I did not want that type of love. I did not want to argue and use the F-word to belittle a person.

"Of course, Dad. Thanks for the ice cream," I replied, eating my cone.

A couple days later, everyone in the house behaved normally as if nothing happened, especially Karen and Dad. Tessa had taken to ignoring the incident. I assumed it was a trait she inherited from her mom, acting completely normal to forget the incident, though I doubted that Tessa deliberately ignored mentioning it. She was too young to make intentional decisions. Nevertheless, I was cautious not to mention that night again. The house appeared happy and safe for the rest of my holidays.

We continued to go to the beach, the pool, Monterey Aquarium, and visit my cousins in Stockton, California. Despite how busy my summer break was, I was impatient to reach home and reveal Karen's behavior and the fight to my mom.

***

"How was your visit, Nomi?" Mom asked.

"It was great. I went to the beach almost every day and continued my swimming lessons. I'm a shark now, Mom. I can really swim. Next year, I can join Junior Lifeguards." I beamed with a big smile.

Mom looked at me excitedly and continued folding clothes. "Did you see some of your cousins?" she asked.

"Yes, we all had a sleepover."

"Cool. Did you learn anything new?"

"Yeah, I don't want to be in love like Dad's love. He and Karen got into it pretty bad over a dream she had."

"What?" my mom yelped. She dropped the clothes she'd been folding. Her eyes grew wider as I told her the details.

"Yeah, Karen was yelling at Dad while Tessa and I were hiding in the room. When I asked Dad what had happened and why he's with her, he told me she had had a dream that he was going to leave her. He said she's been through a lot and that he loves her. Crazy, don't you think? I never want to be in such a relationship."

My mom listened intently to my ranting, and after the initial look of shock and concern about Dad, I noticed a sly smirk on her face as she finished folding the laundry and moved over to the bed to begin making it.

"Why are you smiling?" I asked mid-way through my explanation of what "love" I never wanted.

"Nothing."

"Oh, tell me."

"Um… nothing much. Only wondering whether or not your dad got into this new marriage too soon." She raised her eyebrows and winked.

I stared at her as she popped the sheets on the bed. "Well, I will go call your dad and make sure nothing else happened."

As my mom walked out of the room, I had a feeling that her smile probably had more to do with me than Dad. I felt my cheeks go warm. It struck me how this was the first time I'd expressed my thoughts or observations about love and relationships to my mom.

"Nothing else happened, Mom," I called after her, in a rather futile attempt at sounding confident.

"Really?" Her head bobbed around the corner of the open door.

"Yes. Dad took us out for an ice cream treat, and everything went back to normal after that."

"Oh," she said in an explicit tone as if she knew exactly how that would have turned out. I had a faint déjà-vu sensation when she stared at me a second longer, and she said, "Great then."

I don't know if my mom ever called Dad, but every summer break was similar to that one. There would be one big blow-up between Dad and Karen, but that would be it. Things would revert to being perfect from the very next day. Life was good. I realized that life has its ups and downs, and I learned to always go with the ups. I decided to focus on the good and never the bad. Very early in my life, I understood that focusing on the bad could only make things worse.

***

Between going back and forth with my parents, life in Las Vegas was good. Growing up in a single parent household, I grew up fast and learned about money, bills, and hustle, quicker than your average adolescent. I watched my mom work three jobs to make ends meet, and my dad go from job to job when he wasn't drumming. The struggle was real when I was with my mom during the school year.

"Mom, why are you working so much? We are okay," I'd plead.

"Naomi, bills have to be paid, and I want you to continue to do all your dance classes and cheerleading. I don't want you to be fast and depending on any boy," she'd explain.

"But Mom, I want you to stay home with me. I don't want to go to Auntie's tonight and go to school from there. I like when you drive me to school," I begged.

"Girl!" Mom exclaimed.

"Please, Mom, please!"

"I have to go to work, but how about I take you with me? You can come, make a pallet on the floor while I clean the office, and then we can come home. That way you will be at home, and I can take you to school in the morning. You want to do that?" Mom shunned in a sarcastic tone.

I made a puppy face and looked down.

I'd almost lost all hope when she smiled and asked, "Do you want to do that?"

Heck yeah.

"Yes! Yes! Yes!" I yelled with joy.

"Okay, Nomi, now you understand that I will be working, right?"

"Yes."

"Okay."

My mom was a janitor. She would clean buildings and offices to earn a living. Once we reached the office she was supposed to clean, I wondered why it needed cleaning. It was spotless already. Nevertheless, I figured I could help her until I was tired, plus it could help her get done faster.

"What can I do, Mom?" I asked.

"You really want to help? You're supposed to be making a pallet and going to bed, little girl."

"I know, but I'm not tired yet," I said. "I want to help."

"Okay, move to the front of the office and start dumping the trash into this bag here." She handed me a big black bag that was large enough to fit me in it; I began working.

There were six cubicles and three big offices. The cubicles had tiny trash bags, and just like at home, there were three new mini trash bags ready for you to put in the trash cans. I smiled because I not only had to take the trash out of the bin, but I had to put a bag in there too. *Just like home.*

I never cared for chores, but my mom would say, "You gotta learn this so you can start doing it yourself and grow up and be independent. You think Mommy gonna be around alllll the time to wash your clothes and clean up after you?"

I always looked at her with my "whatever" face and continued my chores at that given time.

"Okay, Mom, I'm done. I dumped the trash and put new bags in all the trash cans. Can we go now?" I said with an accomplished grin on my face.

"No, but you can go lie down now," my mom replied.

"Fine!"

Disappointed, I made my pallet under a desk in one of the cubicles with nothing in it. Before I knew it, I drifted into sleep.

I awoke when cold air hit my face. Mom was trying hard not to walk too loudly up the stairs with me in her arms. She was about 5'2," and I was almost as tall as her. At a vertical incline, it must have been tough carrying me up the stairs.

"Mom…"

"Go back to sleep, Nomi; we're home. I only gotta open the door," she whispered.

"I gotta pee, Mom."

"Hold it!" she said as she propped me up on her left knee to balance me on it, then unlocked the door.

When she put me down, I practically sleepwalked to the toilet. Mom came in and helped me wipe myself, put on my PJs, and walked me to my room.

"Now, go to bed, my Nomi. I love you, and thank you for your help." She kissed me and caressed my hair until we both fell asleep.

Though we struggled, I never went without. Mom always found a way. The struggle seemed to be the norm, and California was my vacation, and I guess Mom's too. She didn't have to worry about me, nor I – her.

Chapter Four

Oh my goodness, is this blood? Ugh, I got my period!

I was in the eighth grade, and it was right after cheerleading practice. Mom told me I would be becoming a woman soon, but I hadn't expected it to be this soon. I didn't even have any breasts yet. I was still flat-chested without any curves. I looked around at all the other girls I went to school with and how they had grown into their shapes. Some had curvy hips, some had voluptuous breasts, and some had both. I had none.

"Mom, why don't I have anything?" I pouted.

"Girl, please! You will get them. And be happy you're small. Them girls gonna be fat later, watch!" Mom said, leaning into me and waving her finger with a sly smile on her face. I laughed. She had an answer for everything, and when it came to other girls, she would always say, "They're fat or fast."

Now that I had my period and I was a woman, I expected to grow some hips and breasts in a couple months. Soon came summer, and it was the same. Still no hips or breasts, but I had "*the look.*" I was pretty and smart with long, dark brown curly hair – longer if it was straight. I had a golden caramel skin tone, almond brown eyes, and full lips. I stood 4'9" with a flexible cheerleader body. With enough popularity and sass, I was ready to move to my new high school – my zoned high school. All through elementary and junior high, Mom found it best to use my aunt's address after my grandma passed away to keep me in the same zone as my friends and family at school.

By ninth grade, I didn't care about hips and breasts. I guess my mom's words had sunk in: "It'll come."

"So, Naomi, are you going to try out for the freshman cheer squad?" asked a nosy girl in my English class.

"Yes," I responded with sass and attitude.

The girl seemed to be sizing up all the girls who had gone to the freshman meeting for tryouts. I knew some of those girls from local Pop Warner football teams, and that was good because I saw familiar faces. The first couple months of high school were nerve-racking, as I didn't know anyone except for the kids in my neighborhood, and since they were all older than me, I didn't see them much.

"Nomi, how're cheer tryouts going?" Mom asked.

"Good. I think I have a good shot at making it."

"You think? You are going to making it!" she declared, raising her eyebrows. Mom was my biggest cheerleader.

"How's dance class going? Better than Las Vegas Dance Theater?" Mom asked, sitting on the couch.

"It's going well, but the teacher keeps riding me. She asked if I'd danced before, and I said yes, and she said she could tell." I rolled my eyes.

Mom gazed at me proudly, and I knew she was thinking, *Shit, I know my baby good.*

"Well, Nomi, don't let that get you down. She must see something in you. Embrace it."

"Okay, Mom."

The list came out for the freshman cheer team. I'd made it.

I felt so accomplished, as the tryouts had been hard and long. We spent two weeks in tryouts after school. I had to learn two dances and four cheers with jumps. Talk about hell. I did it anyway.

Going through my freshman year, I made many friends, and began to develop more as a young woman. I was finally an A cup and had some booty! My cheer uniform fit like a glove, and I felt sexy and superior to others who weren't a part of the team. My school praised athletes, and they respected the cheerleaders as such too.

By the second quarter of my freshman year, I had a boyfriend. He was tall and had skin like cocoa butter. His eyes were deep and displayed strong passion for me. Plus, he was intelligent, popular, had a playful attitude, and walked me to all my classes. This made me feel special. Our love for each other developed very quickly.

"Naomi, will you come to homecoming with me?"

"Yes," I answered instantly. *Oh my God, I'm going to homecoming my freshman year!*

Deon, my boyfriend, was a well-known freshman. He didn't play any sports; however, he knew everyone around the Vegas Valley. He was active within the community and mentored boys younger than him. I was proud to be his girlfriend.

In the midst of homecoming, Dad returned to Las Vegas. He and Karen had parted ways for good, and he was now ready to focus on himself and on me. He'd gotten a job working as a truck driver and worked side gigs on the weekends as a drummer for some local bands in the Valley. I was proud of him because he was really going after his dream. In the same way, I was proud of Deon. I enjoyed thinking of them on the same level, knowing how they both mattered to me.

"Dad, I have homecoming coming up with Deon."

"Okay," my Dad replied, rolling his eyes and chuckling. He continued, "Okay, and…?"

"Can you take me to get a dress?" I asked. "I need one for the dance."

"Okay, we can do that. Where do we go for a dress?" he said, his eyes lighting up. He was excited to join my quest of finding the right dress. He usually never asked about Deon, but when we went shopping, he had a lot of questions.

"So, this Deon guy, how long have you known him?" he asked, trying to play it cool, but his "Daddy serious" voice was difficult to hide.

"Dad, I've known him since middle school. He was my *phone buddy*, as Mom would put it."

"Phone buddy, huh? Okay. Is your mom okay with you calling him your boyfriend?"

"Yes, Dad. Are you?" I replied, looking at him with a serious smirk on my face.

"No. I think you shouldn't have a boyfriend until you're 40," he chuckled. "That dress is nice."

"Oh, Dad, whatever. And thanks." I laughed and spun around in an all-black one-shoulder gown.

It was perfect. Deon and I agreed that we wanted to keep it classic: black and white.

"This is it, Dad. Let's get this one," I said, jumping up and down.

"Okay, baby, tell the lady to get it ready."

***

The night of homecoming was perfect! We had the limo, the money, and the class. Deon was wearing a sleek black and white suit.

Our parents met us at the dance to get pictures of us getting out of the limo, and Deon was showing out, but everyone loved it. They found it cute, and I didn't mind because I knew I was fine.

"I'm the luckiest man tonight. My girl," Deon said, holding my hand and turning me around so he could get a full look. Everyone laughed.

"Thanks, baby! You looking sharp yourself." I leaned in to kiss his cheek.

We walked into the dance, and it was something I had never imagined. The room was filled with blue, silver, and gold balloons. The DJ was playing "Work It" by Missy Elliott. The ambiance of the room was elegant and welcoming. The chaperones complimented us as soon as we walked in and said, "Y'all enjoy and no funny business." We laughed and made it to the dance floor. It was packed with our friends. Deon and I danced the night away and shared our first kiss while dancing to Usher and Monica's "Slow Jam." It was perfect.

As his lips brushed mine and I reciprocated, there was a tingling sensation all over my body. Like an electric shock, but only excitement surged through. I didn't know how to stop it.

I looked at Deon and whispered, "Sorry, I'm nervous for some reason. I feel weird." He nodded and pulled me closer. He then whispered back, "It's okay. I got you. Want to sit down after this dance or now?"

"After."

We finished our dance and sat down. Deon got me some water, and I gulped the whole glass down. He stared at me while the droplets tumbled down my chin. I felt a warmth rise into my skin, and I observed that his cheeks appeared flustered too.

Noticing my stare, he asked, "Naomi, did you feel that when we kissed?"

"Feel what? I know I was tingling all over," I replied.

"Yeah, me too and my... well..." Deon hesitated.

"What?" I asked, looking concerned.

"Well, Nomi, I got hard," he replied.

Hard? What in the world is hard?

I'd heard of the term before, but I'd never really known what it meant. I found out later that Deon was referring to his penis. I had never seen a penis in real life before. I'd seen kids drawing them but never actually saw one.

"Oh, what do you mean, Deon?" I probed.

"My penis got hard, Naomi," said Deon with a slanted mouth and wide eyes while cocking his head to the side. "You know what I mean now."

"Ha, yes. I got it. You were horny," I said, nodding.

"And I think you were too," he responded.

Leaning down to fix my heel strap, I looked up at him, biting my bottom lip, and nodded. "I guess so. I've never felt like that before."

He knew I was a virgin because he had asked me before, during one of our many phone conversations, if he could be "the one."

"You okay now, babe?" Deon leaned in and kissed me on my forehead. I could see he was changing the subject.

"Yes, let's go dance."

***

It was now the third quarter, and Deon and I were going strong. We explored one another more in our alone time. I learned what a real penis looked and felt like. I learned how to give a hand job and kiss at the same time. I also learned what it meant to be wet and how good it felt to be touched down there. Deon turned me on and made me feel good, and I did the same for him. Innocent play.

One day, Deon was absent from school, and a boy in my advanced English class started talking to me.

"Hey, Naomi, you're looking good today," he said.

I didn't know much about flirting except for what I saw on TV – and Janet Jackson, of course.

I replied, "Thank you."

"So, where is your boyfriend today?"

"Where he needs to be," I responded.

"He ain't come to walk you to class today, and he ain't here now," he said, walking around me.

"I know," I replied, walking around him.

"So, where he at? I'd never let you walk alone. You're too beautiful for that," he grinned.

"Thanks, but no thanks. Boy, you crazy, I gotta go to class," I said, rolling my eyes.

However, deep down, I was highly flattered. I knew one thing for sure; he was an upperclassman. And he found me interesting! *Beautiful*, he'd called me. Well, of course, Deon called me beautiful too. But didn't all boyfriends call their girlfriends that? This guy, though, being an upperclassman, could have gotten any girl he liked. But he liked me. Boy, was I blushing!

When Deon returned to school the next day, I didn't say anything about the other boy flirting with me. I didn't find it necessary because my mom would tell me, "You ain't got to tell your business to everybody; it ain't their concern."

That stuck with me, so Deon never knew.

But later, when Deon was walking me to my classes, I found out through small talk that the boy in my advanced class was a part of Deon's community volunteer group. His name was Alex, and he had a car, a job and was taking night classes at the community college to get ahead and graduate early. I thought it was rather odd that Alex suddenly seemed to make himself known while at the beginning of the school year, he'd never walked our way to any of our classes. I only saw him in the hallways, one or two doors up from my classes and in my English class.

I told my best friend, Courtney, about it, and she said, "He likes you, and maybe to get to you, he has to go through Deon."

She was always reading "Black" books, books about Black relationships or Black love. Hence, I trusted her opinion. I kept an eye on Alex, and one day I told him to stop walking with me and Deon.

He replied, "Okay, but can I drive you home? I just want to talk to you."

I felt a storm of butterflies in my stomach and tingling near my toes. But I didn't know if this would be right. *No, I'm not going to let him have me so easily.*

I turned and walked away from him. It'd been a tempting offer; I wouldn't have to ride the school bus home nor walk to my apartment. Immediately, I regretted it.

But I was probably lucky because he didn't seem to lose interest in me that soon. A few months later, when Deon was absent from school again, I finally took Alex up on his offer.

"So, you finally said yes!" he beamed with exuberance.

"Yeah, you kept nagging me, and you make me feel awkward when you're around me and Deon. I learned a lot about you in our group project, so that's why I feel comfortable with you taking me home now," I explained to Alex.

"Yeah, that Jane Eyre project was dope. I'm using it again for my college course. I'm comparing Jane's life to life today. I've sat and spoken with some friends that were adopted, so my research should be pretty good," Alex explained.

Damn! He is smart and sexy.

Alex was a 5'9" light-skinned Filipino boy with big, round, almond brown eyes and a Caesar fade. He had a smart boy look with a "don't fuck with me" swag.

"Oh, okay, you doing all that! Right on!" I replied, snapping out of my thoughts.

"So, I know I only have this time with you, so let me tell you how I feel," Alex said, taking a deep breath. "I've had a crush on you since the beginning of the school year. I would sit a few rows over and towards the back of the class just so I could see you."

"That's creepy, but continue," I said in a high-pitched voice.

"When I found out you were with Deon, I was like 'dang,' but then I knew it was my fault for not coming to you earlier," Alex said.

"How do you know me and Deon ain't been together?" I said, turning towards him and rolling my eyes.

"I don't, but I'm speaking about now," Alex replied with a smirk on his face. "I ain't asking you to leave him, but I want your time too."

What? It didn't make sense to me.

"What do you mean? I can't cheat on Deon."

"I'm not asking you to cheat on him. I'm asking if I can be your good friend? You won't have to tell Deon anything, and I'll keep my distance in school," Alex explained.

"This is crazy, but for some reason, I'm thinking… Okay, okay, maybe we can be friends," I said out loud to Alex.

I knew it was wrong, but I didn't feel bad. I wasn't going to let Alex into my world like that. He'd never be Deon. But I couldn't help but notice how mature he was compared to Deon. He had a lot of freedom, too. As time went by, Alex and I got closer. He'd take me home sometimes after cheer practice, and we'd go for dinner on days he had off. I started to feel attracted to Alex. I only saw Deon at school and sometimes on the weekends if we were going to see a movie.

Alex continued to play it cool until one night when he dropped me off after our dinner at Olive Garden. He got out of the car as he usually did to walk me to my door, but this time instead of hugging me, he leaned in for an unexpected kiss. He held me close and tongued me down.

That tingling came again, but Deon had taught me to embrace it, so I did. I kissed Alex back. I resisted at first, pushing him away, but then I leaned into him and kissed him back. Our eyes closed, and our mouths moved; I thrusted my pelvis into his, and he pushed right below the curve of my back, pulling me in closer to him. The kiss felt like it lasted forever.

After we were done, he grinned and wiped his hand over his lips. "I should be leaving. I'll see you tomorrow, and thank you."

I replied with a cute giggle, "You're welcome, and thank you for dinner."

Alex kept his word. He always kept his distance at school. And soon, he became my little secret.

We began to explore more of each other.

"Naomi, are you a virgin?" Alex asked me.

"Yes. Are you?"

"No, I had sex once before," he replied.

"Oh, okay. Well, you ain't getting any over here, buddy," I responded quickly.

"I wasn't asking to see if I could be your first. I was asking because you've let me finger you, and it didn't seem like it hurt or anything. You enjoyed it, and there was no blood," Alex explained.

Moment of truth.

"Well, that's because Deon and I have dabbled a little bit, and he's made me bleed by doing that."

"Oh, I see. Okay," Alex said, nodding his head. He leaned across the armrest to kiss me and whispered, "But he don't do it like me."

I smiled and pushed him away, as he asked, "Can I see you tomorrow?"

"Yes."

Deon had no clue, and I didn't say anything. Alex made it easy for me to cheat at this moment. I'd never known what "cheating" meant in relationship terms, but when I asked Mom, she said, "Cheating on a person means you are not with just that one person."

"Why do you ask, Naomi?" she added in her serious yet curious tone.

"I just want to know. I think I'm starting to like Alex, but I have Deon, Mom," I said.

Smiling and gesturing for me to sit next to her, she replied, "Baby, boys are going to come and go. Don't worry about getting serious with these boys. It is okay to like both of them, but if you feel you need to talk to Deon because he's been around longer, talk to him. You'll know what to say."

"Thanks, Mom."

I don't think Mom understood how deep I'd been in. Her idea of me having a boyfriend perhaps meant a friend who was a boy. And about intimacy, I don't think she would appreciate I'd gone beyond holding hands and regular kissing. For me, it was already so much more.

Back at school, Deon got word that he would be moving away to another country at the end of the summer. I was sad but relieved to know I wouldn't have to continue with this burden on me. Come the fourth quarter of the school year, Deon and I were still seeing one another at school and sometimes on the weekends. Alex was still around, too. He and I were getting closer, and I began to let my guard down. By the end of my ninth-grade year, Alex had taken my virginity, and Deon, assuming he was the first, did too.

Knowing that Deon was leaving, I had to make it seem like he was my first. Given that there wasn't any blood because Deon had popped my cherry fingering me. It was easy for me to say he was my first, when in fact, Alex had been my first.

My ninth-grade year taught me that I was smart; I got straight A's, learned the art of flirting, played hard to get, got to know my body, and learned how to kiss and how to lie. Deon left that summer going into my tenth-grade year, never knowing he was my second body – yet first love. Alex and I remained friends, but he transferred to the community college to finish his last year.

CHAPTER FIVE

When tenth grade began, I was single. Since I'd had an eventful ninth grade, I wanted tenth grade to be a lot smoother. I'd already lost my virginity, dated two boys simultaneously, and learnt everything I could about flirting and falling "in love." However, I never let anything, or anyone, come in between me and my studies. My parents always stressed education, as they didn't have much education themselves. They wanted better for me. Tenth grade was the year to make it count because colleges were now on the radar. Therefore, I made a pact: no boys and no more relationships.

However, my "oh-so-nice girl" pact didn't last long. I met someone special in tenth grade that piqued my interest. Gerald was an eleventh grader from a different school, and I met him through a friend at a party. We became phone buddies and learned a lot about one another. One weekend we met up to go swimming at my friend's place, and that's when I learned about receiving pleasure and giving pleasure. Gerald taught me how to understand my body and what it meant to have an orgasm. He taught me not to be shy about my body and that my curves are my weapon. He'd always say, "Naomi, it's your eyes and your smile that gets me to do whatever you want me to do for you."

We agreed that if we were going to mess around, we mustn't catch feelings because we didn't want to be in a relationship. Days went by, and I enjoyed my time with Gerald. He was the bad boy who treated me like the badass girl I deserved to be. I loved when he showered me with compliments about my body in a nonchalant way. He made me feel sexy, like a Goddess. The way he'd look at me sometimes reminded me of how that man had looked at Janet Jackson. And that look was priceless.

When I was with Gerald, our sex was great. We explored various kinks and fetishes. His attitude was one of a kind, and I felt safe with him. I knew I could depend on him, but there were no emotions involved. This "no-strings-attached" feeling is what made my connection with Gerald special.

I was happy with how things were going, and never for one moment did I question if I wanted more – until one day when I met another guy at the movies. This new guy was different. It only took a few days for me to realize he was my Prince Charming. So, I decided to be upfront and tell Gerald about him.

Gerald was "The Guy" in my life, the one guy I could tell anything and everything and the only one who taught me to be bad in a sexy kind of way. We'd always been open and honest with each other. Therefore, when I told him about Rodney, the new guy I had met at the movies, Gerald was quite supportive.

"I really like this new guy," I said.

"Okay, so what are you saying?" Gerald asked.

"Well, I've been talking to him for a while now, and he asked me to be his girlfriend. I haven't given him an answer yet because I'm messing around with you," I explained.

"Soooo, do you want to be with that dude?"

"Honestly, I want you, but I know our agreement. Plus, you are going through hard times at the moment."

"Are you telling me that either we be together or we are done?"

"No, I'm telling you that we are done. No more messing around." I said it out loud and regretted it the very next moment.

Dang! He was everything. Good dick, good looks, good conversations. Oh well.

But a part of me craved to be with someone who truly wanted me and not just an arrangement, so I became Rodney's girlfriend.

"Naomi, I really like you. We talk every day, fall asleep on the phone together, and we even live near one another. Will you be my girlfriend?" Rodney again asked over the phone one night.

"Yes! About time you asked again!" I said happily, yelling into the phone.

Rodney stood 6'3" with a caramel complexion and broad shoulders. He had a hooper's body, and he would pick me up and twirl me around. I was falling!

Until then, I'd only known the love I felt for my family and friends, but this love with Rodney was different. He made me feel alive. Like, I was his everything. Our first time was epic! I felt sparks as if our bodies were fireworks bursting as one big grand finale. From that moment on, we were inseparable.

Rodney was the only child living at home, as he had older siblings, but he never saw them, so he was treated as such. Since I was the only child too, we managed to do a lot because we received pretty big allowances for our age. Combined, we made $100 a week. That was a lot. When he could get the car from his parents, we would go to Red Lobster and enjoy the Seafood Trio. At times, we'd drive over to Olive Garden and enjoy the amazing pasta. We'd enjoy long walks in the park and gaze at the city lights from Hollywood Drive, a place situated atop the Vegas Valley mountain that I considered no less than a paradise.

Soon, the time came for me to take my driving license test, and I was nervous.

"This is the moment we have been working towards, Naomi," Dad said. "Remember when you went for your permit test at the beginning of the year?"

"Yes, Dad."

"It's the same thing. The only difference here is that you will be driving with someone in your car. And it still stands, if you don't pass, it's gonna be a lonnnnng ride home because you won't get your car that daddy bought for you," Dad said in a slow, irritating yet teasing voice.

"I know, Dad. I got this. I'm just driving someone around. I'll imagine it's you. You taught me everything I know, Dad. I love you!" I said, embracing him with a big hug and a peck on the cheek.

"Naomi, you ready?" an old man said, walking up to us. "I'll be your examiner today. Let's get started, shall we?"

"Okay, see ya soon, Dad," I said before walking out of the DMV doors to the car.

Once the test was over, the old man looked at me and said, "Well, happy birthday, Naomi! You passed. You can officially turn in your permit to me and go to desk number 9. I'll forward all your paperwork to the lady there. Just give her your name."

"Oh my goodness! Yayy me! Thank you, sir." I ran back into the DMV yelling for Dad.

"DAD! I DID IT! I DID IT! I PASSED, AND I GET MY CAR NOW!" I screamed and hugged him.

"Yayy! Daddy's baby! I knew you could do it. And yes, yes, yes, you get to officially have your car now," he said, embracing me and kissing my forehead.

He yelled out to the rest of the DMV, "MY BABY PASSED, Y'ALL! SHE CAN DRIVE NOW WITHOUT ME."

On the way home, Dad let me drive, and he gave me his rules for driving on my own.

Dad, whatever, you've allowed me to drive to school on my own, and Mom lets me go to the store on my own when I didn't have a license. So why you all "ruley" now?

"Okay, Dad. Don't worry," I said, cutting him off in the middle of his rule-giving.

"Baby, Daddy is serious. You aren't just driving to school or the store anymore. You have all of Vegas to roam now. Stay aware and be safe! And don't be having that boy Rodney in your car!" He chuckled at the last part.

Dad didn't care for Rodney. He knew I was falling in love with Rodney, and when I told him how I felt about Rodney, he seemed sad and uncomfortable. Perhaps it was because I was discussing a boy with him and with such passion.

"Dad, I think I really like Rodney."

"Oh, how do you know?" he said.

"Well, Dad, he makes me smile, and he gives me flowers. He always knows when I've done something to my hair, and his hugs are warm," I replied.

"Oh really, he notices and does all that? How're his parents?"

"They're cool. They like me," I said.

"Has your mom met his parents?"

"Yes. They all met right before Fall Formal. Uncle Steven met them all too," I shared.

"Oh, okay, that's right. I was out of town," Dad said, remembering the time.

Dad was very protective of me, but he knew I was smart – though not quite in the way I thought of the term. When he gave me the talk about the birds and the bees, it was very different from the way Mom had discussed it with me. He'd told me a story.

"Baby, now that you are getting older, it's time for you to choose who you want to be. Do you want to be the girl who winds up pregnant at a young age and tries to manage school and work and get a babysitter? Or do you want to be the girl who goes through school, gets a career, lives her life, and settles down on her terms? These are the choices that life will throw at you. Be smart. Be sharp," he finished and kissed my forehead. "Daddy loves you."

I didn't say much after the story, but after giving it some thought, I replied, "I am Naomi, the girl who goes through school, gets a career, lives her life to the fullest, of course, and settles down, if I so choose to, with someone that loves me for me."

"That's right! Shoots!" Dad replied, walking like George Jefferson from the TV show *The Jeffersons*. We laughed, but he knew, much like I knew, that we'd been serious.

Chapter Six

By eleventh grade, Rodney and I were still in love with each other. He was now a high school senior and had started his quest to apply to colleges. All he wanted to do was hoop and be an artist. He went to a gifted and talented school for his artistry.

"Bae, let me paint you. I want to paint you just like this," he said one day after sex.

"What? No, Bae. That is risky. What if someone finds it?" I asked.

"No one will. It'll be part of our private collection," he said.

"Okay, fine." I rolled my eyes and followed it with a nervous and excited grin, biting my bottom lip. *Imma be Rose from Titanic.* I laughed to myself.

Right when I thought he'd been joking, he got up and returned with a pencil and paper and began to sketch me. He looked at me with piercing eyes, and the calm, determined expression on his face sent a tingling sensation down my back. After a few weeks, Rodney had achieved it. He'd painted a portrait of me naked. He captured my passion-filled eyes, the sweat beads trickling down my neck to my breasts; my plump lips and my aroused body beamed in the picture. From that day forward, I saw myself as a Goddess.

As the year went on, Rodney and I became more and more involved in each other's lives. We did everything together. I was beginning to think I'd found my soulmate until we went to this one party, and I saw "The Guy."

"Gerald," I called out to him before I could think.

He turned around and beamed like we were still together. That's what I loved most about him. I returned his smile and began a bit of small talk. We were only minutes into this conversation when Rodney approached us with an uptight face. He'd seen us make an acquaintance, and shockingly to me, he looked furious.

He stared at me with stealthy, narrow eyes and asked, "Who's this, Bae?"

Before I could answer, Gerald replied in his usual nonchalant tone, "The nigga who let her be with you."

Gerald had evidently picked up on the superior tone of Rodney's voice, and I knew he wasn't the type of guy who'd tolerate something like this. His retort very well complemented his personality and what I knew about him. But what took me by surprise was my boyfriend's reaction.

"What, nigga?" Rodney glared at him and roughly turned towards me. "Nomi, who is this guy?"

I was completely taken aback by the sudden anger and doubt in his voice. His facial muscles pulled into a tight, thin expression and his lower lip trembled with jealousy. I opened my mouth to explain, but no voice came out. I was too shocked.

Rodney grabbed my arm and rushed me out of the party. I tried explaining while stumbling to make it through the crowd. "Bae, he is someone I used to talk to. Nothing serious. I promise. I know him from back in the day."

"Why is this nigga talking about '*letting you*' be with me? What the fuck is that?" Rodney blurted with his chest all puffed up.

My heart was beating fast. I was scared. And all I could do was cry. I didn't have any words to say.

I can't tell Rodney who "The Guy" really is. If I say any more, this nigga is going to be mad, and then I don't know what he may do next. He'll flip even more.

I remained quiet and wept. He looked at me a second more, and his face somewhat softened.

"Naomi, don't cry," he said. "I'm just upset. I saw you talking to him and hugging him. And then, when I inquired, he was straight disrespectful, and his eye contact with me made me think some sneaky-ish was going on."

Crying and shaking now, I replied, "He's just an old friend, that's all. You're scaring me."

"I'm sorry," he said, kissing me. "I'm sorry."

I kissed him back and pulled him closer. "Let's just go."

Back then, it could have been considered a casual couple fight. But that night, I saw a side of Rodney that I never wanted to see again. The way he grabbed me was nothing I ever expected from him. He hurt me and left a bruise on my left arm. When he saw it, he couldn't believe he had done that to me. He apologized until the bruise disappeared.

I wasn't sure if I was scared of him or not. I knew deep down we were starting to grow apart because I realized he was slowly becoming more skeptical of everyone I would hang around with, especially guys. His skepticism reached a point where I stopped hanging with my friends completely and began hanging out with him and his friends. That, too, began to wear on me, and soon enough, there was a rebellious streak growing inside of me. I started hanging with my friends again and going to girl outings. During that time, Rodney and I saw less of each other, and after a few months, my life came crumbling down. I found out that Rodney had cheated on me with another girl. She was beautiful. She had chocolate butter skin with high cheek bones, full hips and voluptuous breasts, and reminded me of everything I was not. I couldn't help feeling utterly insulted by the very person I loved the most. And worst of all, I thought it was my fault.

Should I have not started hanging back out with my friends? Should I have given him more attention? Did he not like my body? Maybe I am just not enough for him. These questions and thoughts started to flood my mind.

"Rodney, what happened? Why? Why did you do it?" I asked with tears in my eyes.

"Naomi, it was a mistake. You weren't around, and she was there. She is a family friend, and I've known her since we were kids. I'm sorry," Rodney said.

"The fuck! Nigga, are you serious right now? You get jealous over a nigga at a party saying hi to me, and you go fuck another chick because you been knowing her? And then you have the audacity to hide it from me? I had to find out through a text message she sent you, complimenting you about your house?! You think that's a cool thing for your girlfriend to find out? Get the fuck out of here!"

I could feel my ears getting hot and my fists balling up. I began to cry. "I can't believe you did this to me, to us. I ain't done nothing to you but be good to you. Why, Rodney, why?"

He stayed quiet and tried to embrace me. I began pounding his chest with my balled fists, screaming out at him. He held me tightly until my body relaxed, and he started to kiss me. I did not kiss back. He continued to smother me with kisses, sliding down, unbuttoning my jeans, and all I could do was cry. I felt like I was in the movie *Baby Boy*; he was Jody, and I was Yvette.

That night, I stayed over at his house. In the morning, I woke up feeling dumb.

What the fuck, Naomi? This is not cool! He cheats and gets a pass because he gives you oral? No, don't be that girl. Don't be like your dad and Karen.

"Rodney, wake up," I said, tapping him on the shoulder.

"What's up, Bae?"

"I can't do this. We can't be together. What you did hurt my feelings," I said.

"Bae, no, please don't leave me. I don't know what I'd do without you. Please, baby, don't leave me," he pleaded and began to cry.

When he began to shed tears, it was at that moment when I believed he was sorry. I didn't care what he'd done anymore. My heart began to feel warm, and his emotion made me feel like he truly cared about us. About me.

And I stayed in the relationship. Somewhere, inside my mind, it started to make sense why my dad had stayed with Karen.

He loved her. I loved Rodney.

Chapter Seven

My twelfth-grade year came around, and it was the year of finals. Final dance competitions, final cheer competitions, final homecoming and fall formals, final prom – the final year of being watched over by adults. I was coming into my adulthood. This was my final year for any fuck-ups.

Rodney had gone to college in another state. We (I mean, I) made a conscious effort to see each other every other weekend. Our relationship never got back to what it was, but I learned to get even instead of getting mad. We were the perfect couple to our families, but we were toxic for one another to our friends. He'd cheat; I'd break up with him and date another nigga until he came back or until I missed him. That had become our routine, and anyone else involved understood their place.

"Naomi, girl, wake up. I got to tell you something," yelled my homegirl over the phone one night.

"I'm up," I replied groggily. "What's going on?"

"It's Rodney," she explained. "Girl, he is here at my school's dance."

"WHAT! Are you serious?!"

"Girl, yes! He's with another girl, and they are looking very cozy! What you gonna do?"

"Nothing. Fuck him," I said, trying to hide the crack in my voice.

I felt my heart break into tiny pieces. Now that my girls knew about his betrayal, I was embarrassed. I hung up and cried myself to sleep. After that night, I kept getting calls from my friends informing me about Rodney's whereabouts and which new girl he had on his arm.

A few days later, when I couldn't take it anymore, I decided to cease my silent treatment and drive down to Arizona State University. Pushing 108 miles per hour, the highway patrol stopped me.

Walking up slowly and shining his light into my car's tinted windows, the officer asked me to roll my window down.

"Evening, young lady. Do you know why I've stopped you tonight?"

"Yes, sir. I was speeding. I'm sorry, I must have let my rage get the best of me," I replied.

"Rage? Now, what got you all upset? Can I see your license and registration, please?"

"Officer, my boyfriend, who I've been with for years, is cheating on me, and I'm hurt. So, I am going to confront him now."

"Well, your license shows that you're not 18 yet. You're a month shy of your birthday, young lady. Are you in school? It is a school night," the officer said.

Thinking on my toes, I cooked up a lie. "Yes, I'm in school, but I'm a senior, so I only attend classes Monday through Thursday. We have block schedules at my school. My mother is aware of my travel. Would you like to call her?" I offered with confidence I lacked within.

"No, that will not be necessary. I swear schooling is different from when I went to school. But I am going to have to give you a ticket for your speeding," explained the officer.

"I understand. I will take care of it, I promise. And thank you for stopping me. I could have hurt someone," I said, heaving a sigh of relief. Lying to the police was no cakewalk.

Laughing a jolly laugh, the officer replied, "Now, go confront that cheating boyfriend of yours, but watch your speed. Have a good evening, young lady."

***

"Rodney!" I yelled while banging on his door. "Open this fucking door before I kick it in."

"Bae, what's wrong? Why you tripping? You ain't been answering my calls. Did your phone get taken away again? I know we ain't go over our minutes. We talk for free," Rodney yelled back through the door before opening it, not sure if he should be happy or scared.

When he opened the door, I walked towards him and swung my right hook into his ribs.

"I know about that girl, and I'm done. You can go and fuck her! And I also know about her being pregnant and having an abortion for you. You hella stupid! You thought I'd never find out? I am glad I got loyal friends. Unlike your unloyal ass!"

I pounded on his chest with my fists and elbows, alternating my swings – right hook, left hook, push and push....

"Bae, I swear I ain't get that girl pregnant. She is lying!" he claimed.

"Oh, really? Okay, so if she lying, call her and tell her then," I replied, handing him the phone.

He pushed it out of my hands and tried to restrain me. I kicked my legs until he put me down, and then I began elbowing him in the ribs and stomach. Initially, he tried to reason with me for a few minutes, but once he realized that I did indeed know everything, he slammed me down on the floor and put his weight on me.

That fueled my anger like never before, and I screamed out, "That's why I've fucked with other people too! Get off me!"

"You bitch!" he growled, and I knew I'd said the wrong thing.

Instead of backing off, he began to slap me.

Why did I say that shit? I cursed myself.

We fought hard that night, and needless to say, my plan of cursing him out and getting revenge ended with both of us being hurt and bruised. I remained in Arizona for the weekend and told Mom that I was at my friend's house, which would have been true, but our fight had gotten the best of us. We fought Friday night, didn't talk Saturday, and made up that Sunday before I drove home.

"I love you, Naomi. I promise I'll make it right," Rodney said, leaning in to kiss me. "I'll pay for your speeding ticket. I don't want your dad being mad at you for sneaking out of town, or me," Rodney urged.

"Okay. I love you too, Rodney," I replied.

However, that day, I was over Rodney and the way he treated me. I reciprocated his "I love you" not because I loved him or expected him to keep the promise, but because I didn't want to fight anymore. This had become our pattern: argue, fight, makeup and say nice things, or we'd fuck. I always felt like I was in a movie scene every time we had a toxic fight. We'd fight and have make-up sex. This was us. And I was definitely not proud of us anymore. This was our pattern, and I was over it. His dick was good, but I'd realized I deserved better.

Back at school, everything was normal until I got a blast from the past. My girls and I were out at a house party and there I saw him again. Gerald, *the nigga who "let" me be with Rodney.*

I felt a surge of emotions rush through me. He was The Guy in my life, or at least he had been. The one person I never felt insecure with.

I took a deep breath and approached him. Again, as if nothing had ever changed between us, he smiled at me and began small talk.

"Hey, Naomi baby! How's your final year of high school treating you?" he asked.

"I'm not your baby," I smiled, "but it's going well. I can't complain. How's life for you, Mr. '*I ain't in high school anymore*' ass?" I asked in a flirtatious manner.

"It's good, a nigga just working and doing this trade school shit," he replied in a nonchalant, swaggy manner.

"Oh, okay, that's what's up. It's been a minute."

"Yeah, it has. You still with ol' dude?" he asked – the one question I was hoping he wouldn't ask.

"Yeah, I am," I replied, dropping my head.

"You are?" he asked curiously, but there wasn't any judgement in his voice or on his face.

Looking up at him, I grinned and raised my eyebrow. "Yes, but he ain't here."

"I see that." He smirked the smirk I knew very well. "Tell your girls you 'bout to go. Have one of them take your car. I'll drop you off later."

He leaned in and lightly brushed his lips on mine. His long arm enveloped me as I caught the whiff of his familiar scent, and a burst of all the memories of him treating me like the badass girl returned to my senses.

"Okay," I replied with a wide grin on my face before I walked out with him. Any embarrassment or insecurity I'd felt with Rodney disappeared. That night, with Gerald, I truly embraced my body.

***

It was February. The trees were bare, the air was crisp, and the wind was cold. The only warmth in the surroundings came from the sun. My senior year was going great. Rodney and I seemed to be on good terms, and I had started getting college acceptance letters. Life was good.

Gerald was officially out of my life, as he'd run into some legal issues in January that got him locked up for a couple of years. Until he got locked up, I would go chill with him when Rodney and I were on bad terms. He knew it too, but he never questioned it.

All was well until the end of February when I realized I'd missed my period. I didn't give it much thought at first because I'd always been irregular. Then, when March ended, and there was still no sign of Auntie Flo, I began panicking. I called one of my homegirls and told her what could be going on.

"Tina, I think I'm pregnant," I blabbered as soon she answered her phone.

"Did you get a pregnancy test?"

"Not yet, but I haven't had my period."

"Okay, I'll go to Walmart and get two. You can come over to my house and take'em," she said, trying to hide the worry in her voice.

When I reached Tina's house, she was ready with the tests.

"I'm scared," I said. "What if I am really pregnant? Coach is not going to be happy with me."

"Just take it first, and we can figure it out from there," Tina replied, leading me into the bathroom.

Once inside and alone, I opened the box and scuffled through the papers, pulling the wrapped stick out. Ripping the wrapper off the test stick and taking a deep breath, I relieved myself.

Three minutes later, two pink lines appeared. PREGNANT!

My heart dropped into my stomach.

Tina suggested I take the second test to be sure, and the results were the same.

What am I going to do? I was terrified.

Pacing back and forth, I tried to calm myself down. "Naomi, you got this. You can fix this," I said aloud.

"Have you and Rodney ever thought about what y'all would do if you got pregnant?" Tina asked.

"Yes, we said we would abort if I ever got pregnant, as we both value our education, and we'd be going to different colleges," I replied.

"Okay, so now where do you go to get an abortion?" Tina asked.

"How the fuck am I supposed to know, Tina?" I shouted, and she immediately went quiet.

"Oh, I'm sorry," I said after a while. "I know you are only trying to help, but I'm not able to think of anything right now."

"It's all right, Nomi." She pulled me in for a hug. "I understand how hard it can be. I'm here for you. And well, you know what, let me call my God mama. I guess she'll advise us better."

Tina's God mama was very cool and open-minded. She'd always been there for us and never judged us when we spoke to her about sex. She'd always say, "Just be sure you ladies use protection." The idea of taking advice from her calmed me down a little, and I nodded.

Once Tina got off the phone, she said, "Naomi, my God mama said we got to go to the clinic first and confirm your pregnancy. They'll be able to tell you how many weeks you are. Then, we can google a private abortion clinic. She said a private clinic would be the safest as they are usually private OB/GYNs."

"Okay. I'll go tomorrow morning. I'm free then," I said.

"Want me to go with you?" Tina offered.

"No, I'll go. You need to go to school," I replied dimly.

That night, sleep didn't come to me. I kept tossing and turning in my bed, worrying about everything else that could go wrong. I fell asleep in the wee hours and was troubled by horrific nightmares of me with a large baby bump, crying in front of my dad. In my dream, the pregnant Naomi looked weak, tired, and somewhat old and weeping. She said, "I'm sorry, Dad, I became the girl who gets pregnant young and fails at everything."

Dad turned towards me; his eyes were hollow, and his face carried an emotionless expression. "You've let me down, Naomi."

I woke up gasping loudly. I was safe, healthy, and in my bed. After a while, my rapid breathing normalized. *No, I won't let this get to me.*

The next morning, I got up as usual and started my day. I couldn't bring myself to reveal my pregnancy to Mom. I didn't want to disappoint her, and after the nightmare last night, I couldn't tell my dad. He'd be super upset and would probably kill Rodney. I always found it easy to talk to my parents about anything. I always wanted them to know what was going on with me, but I never wanted to upset them. I never wanted them to feel as if they'd failed as parents. I know I was their pride and joy, so I kept it to myself.

Arriving at the clinic as soon as it opened, I followed the crowd in. I asked the information desk for further instructions if I wanted to get a pregnancy test done. The receptionist looked at me shrewdly, as if guessing my age. I shifted uncomfortably under her gaze. *And here it begins.*

She handed me a sheet of paper and pointed to a door with the sign "General Clinic."

"Fill this out, take this number, and they'll let you know the process," she said, pretending to be nonchalant, but her curious, beady eyes gave her away.

I walked quickly through the door and took a seat among many other waiting patients. I sat there, filling out the sheet and ready to cry.

I wish Rodney was here. I hadn't told Rodney about the pregnancy just yet. I wanted to be sure first and know the facts.

"Number 157!" a nurse from the front desk called out.

I hurried over. "Yes, that's me."

"I need to see your ID. You're here for a pregnancy test?" the nurse asked, gazing at the paper without looking up at me. I liked her calm voice.

"Okay, here's my ID, and yes, I'm here to find out if I am pregnant and how many weeks I may be."

"Sure. Please understand that we can do the test, but the weeks can be off by one week or so. You would need to go to your OB/GYN to get an exact date."

"Okay, I can do that."

"How will you pay? Cash or credit? It's $50."

"Pay? I don't have any money on me," I said, and she looked up, eyeing me closely. This wasn't a stare of judgement. She smiled warmly.

"No problem, dear. Fill this sheet out, and it'll be free for you," she said in a soothing voice that eased my worries a bit. She had me fill out a paper for people who "claimed" they didn't have any money. The form had a checklist asking why I didn't have money. I checked a box saying that I was unemployed and living with a family member.

"Thank you," I said, submitting the form.

"Okay, Naomi, go have a seat, and they'll call you by your number when it is time for you to go to the back," the nurse explained.

After waiting 30 minutes, I was called to the back.

"Hi, Naomi, I'll be your doctor today." She was a sweet old lady with black hair and purple nails.

I smiled weakly at her.

"I need you to take this cup here, go to the bathroom and urinate in it. Once you are done, you'll see a panel with a door on the right. Put your sample there and return to this room."

I got up nervously and did as she instructed.

Once back in the room, the doctor came in and asked, "Do you know when your last period was?"

"Yes, January 12th."

"All right, let me input that here," she said, turning to her computer. "Well, Naomi, you are pregnant. You're about six and a half weeks pregnant."

My heartbeat slowed for a second before rocketing up again. *No! It happened.*

I began to cry.

"Oh, oh, Naomi." The doctor came over to my side and put a gentle hand on my shoulder. "What's the matter, hun? There's nothing to be worried about."

"Doctor, I feel bad for asking, but do you know of any abortion clinics? I do not want to go through with this pregnancy. I'm in my senior year of high school," I explained in between sobs.

Looking at me with care and concern, the doctor replied, "That's all right, hun. It's your choice whether or not you want to go through with the pregnancy. I'd suggest googling 'Abortion Clinic on Sahara.' It is a private doctor's office."

I nodded and wiped my tears away. Leaving the clinic, I felt sick to my stomach. I couldn't believe I had been so stupid as to get knocked up by such a dumbass! Or could it be… *Oh my God!*

My head spiraled as the thought flooded through my veins. The last time I'd slept with Rodney had been before Christmas. And according to the calculations the doctor had revealed, I had to have gotten pregnant sometime around… the house party! *Gerald!!*

I couldn't believe it.

Why did it have to happen now when Gerald was finally out of the picture? Ugh, fuck my luck. And ah, shit, what do I tell Rodney?

> Dear Gerald,
>
> I know it's been a while since we've talked, and I haven't been answering your calls or letters, but a lot has been going on since you left. I am pregnant. The baby is yours, but I am not keeping it. Rodney has no idea, and I plan to keep it that way. This will be my last letter to you. I thought I should let you know. I wish you all the best on your next trial.
>
> Take care,
>
> Naomi.

A week went by after sending the letter, and Gerald called me. Of course, I expected the call, as I knew he would want to keep the baby.

"Naomi, baby, I got your letter. It was short and to the point. I understand that you may be feeling scared and alone. I'm sorry for that, but please don't get rid of our baby. I love you, and I will do better once I'm out," Gerald pleaded.

"Gerald, I can't. How the fuck do you expect me to wait without being sure if you'll be out or not? I can't risk it. Plus, I'm scared. You know I start college in the fall."

"Just think about it. I'll have my mom call you," he replied.

"No, you won't. I'm done. Bye!"

Click. I threw the phone aggressively across my bed.

I guess it's time for me to tell Rodney.

He was still in Arizona, and we barely talked, but I had to let him know. I felt guilty for having to lie about some calculations to make him believe it was his baby, but I needed him nevertheless. I was desperate. Summer was approaching fast, and I didn't have much time or money to get the procedure done.

"Hello!" Rodney answered, sounding pleased to hear from me.

"Hey, you busy?" I asked.

"No, just playing the game. What's up, you good?"

"Yes and no. We gotta talk," I began, not ignoring the nervous ting of my voice. "Rodney, I'm pregnant," I said and waited for his reaction.

"Oh, alright," he said casually as if it was an everyday occurrence. "You'll get an abortion, right?"

I was appalled at the calmness and the lack of shock or disbelief in his voice. It was disturbing. *How normal could this sound to him?* And then my mind was flooded with thoughts of all his previous flings and the "other girl" he had gotten pregnant. *So, I'm just one of them now?*

I took a sharp breath. *I am not going to let him affect me. Not anymore.*

"Hello? Naomi? You there?" His voice pounded in my ears.

"Yes, yes," I replied, coming to my senses. "I am sticking to our plan of abortion, but that takes money."

"Alright. How much? And how far along are you?"

"It's $570, but I'm almost in my second trimester. I'm about nine and a half weeks now. The clinic says that once I hit my second trimester, 12 weeks, the price goes up every week by a couple hundred dollars."

"A'ight, can we wait till I'm home, so I'm there with you? I'd prefer if I'm there, so you're not alone," he said.

"Okay, but you know I'll be well into my second trimester by then."

"I know. I'll get the money. Have you told your parents?" Rodney asked.

"No."

"Good. We'll get through this," Rodney encouraged me.

"Okay, well, I'm 'bout to go to bed. I love you," I said.

"I love you too, and don't worry," Rodney said in a gentle voice.

***

April was approaching fast, and my belly wasn't showing, but I felt like shit on the inside. Keeping such a big secret from my parents was killing me, and not having the required funds was daunting.

"Nomi, baby, what's wrong?" Mom asked.

"Nothing, Mom. The finals are getting to me, and graduation is right around the corner," I replied in a stressed voice. I was tired, and I couldn't face her because of my recent lies.

I went to my room and closed the door. I was becoming a hermit crab. I didn't want to be around anyone. My friends who knew what was going on tried to keep my spirits up, but I fell deeper into this depression. I didn't want to go to school. I didn't want to perform nor be seen by anyone. Gerald kept sending letters to check on me, but I threw them away. My bad decision was eating away at me.

Maybe if I don't eat, I'll lose the baby, and I'll be fine, or I can go to the fair this weekend and – oops. Nomi, think! How can I make this an accident, or better yet, how do I make money to get my abortion? I pondered hard over it, making a list of all the people in my circle with some decent money. Then I reached out to one of my girlfriends, Monica, and asked her about her job. She worked in the mall, but she always had money.

"Hey, girl. How you doing?" Monica answered the phone.

"Girl, I'm in hell. I need a job, and I need money now." I laughed nervously and went quiet.

"Well, my job isn't hiring, but I have a weekend job that's hiring. Let's get together Friday night, and I can show you where I work," she offered.

"Cool. I'll meet you at your place, and we can go."

Feeling a bit relieved, I managed school that week. Rodney was going to be home in May, so the time for my abortion was drawing nearer. I was 15 weeks now, and my stomach was still flat, but if I relaxed, it'd pudge out a bit. I kept sucking my stomach in. Finally, Friday night came, and I met up with Monica.

She stood 5'8" with long black hair and a slender face. Her body had curves, and she could speak French and Spanish. She was confident and had sex appeal. We used to perform together at the Las Vegas Dance Theatre when we were younger, but as time went on and we grew up, we became distant friends.

"Nomi, where we're going will only be between me and you, okay?" Monica stared dead into my eyes.

"Girl, you acting like we going to a dope house!" I laughed, and she followed suit.

As we drove down into the Valley, I noticed we were driving on the back roads near the adult stores and strip clubs. We parked at a club. The parking lot had many potholes, and the sign was barely lit. I couldn't make out if we were at a strip club, bar, or an adult store.

It was an off-white building that looked abandoned and needed tending to. Its outside walls had holes where the stucco had come off or was just worn by the weather. As I followed Monica into the building, the smell of bleach, cigarettes, and sweet body mist filled the air. Through the first set of doors was a small adult store that seemed like it didn't get any business. We continued to walk through to the back of the store and through another set of doors.

Through these doors, I stepped into another world. I heard loud music and the lights kept getting dimmer and soon turned red. As the room opened up and we walked through, I saw brass poles, money, men, titties, and ass all over the place.

"Naomi, close your mouth!" Monica smirked.

My eyes were wide open, and so was my jaw. "What in the world?"

"This is where I work on the weekends," she giggled.

"Oh wow! Okay…" I said, surprised.

I'd never been to a strip club before, and even being in this place felt like a sin to my younger self. It was taboo. But some part of me tickled with excitement at witnessing what I'd only ever imagined in my craziest fetishes. I inhaled the musky smell of the air and breathed lightly, my eyes wandering over everyone and everything.

"They're hiring. You're 18, so you're legal to work here. And no one will ever know, Naomi. This can be between us. Also, we go to different schools, so it'll be cool to work together and chill here, like the old days." Monica beamed with excitement.

I didn't know what to say. As much as I was surprised about being there, working at this place seemed out of context to me. But in the daze of such risqué-ness, I stayed quiet and nodded.

"Great. I'll go get my boss. Have a seat. I'll be right back." Monica hopped away.

I sat down and gave myself a pep talk.

Naomi, just think of this as an improv dance class. Make your money and get out! I need this abortion before fall. What do I tell my parents? Oh, I got a waitressing job at the 18+ club that just opened… Yeah, that'll work. I can do this… Damn, I can't do this… What if someone sees me? What do I do? No one will see me. I'll be okay. Shoots! Monica ain't been seen. This place is very low-key. I can do this. Get the money and get out!

"Hey, love, come over to the back and chat with me." A tall white woman who looked like a blowup doll came around. Her voice was sexy and chalklike. I couldn't help noticing the artificial tone. I got up and followed her to her office.

"How old are you?" she asked.

"Eighteen."

"Have you ever danced before?" the lady asked.

"Yes. I'm classically trained."

She chuckled and clarified her question. "Have you ever danced exotically before?"

"No. This would be my first time," I answered bashfully.

"That's not a problem. Are you still in school?"

"Yes. I graduate this June," I replied.

"I'll need you to work Friday and Saturday nights and Sunday, day shift. Can you do that?" the lady asked.

"What are the timings?"

"Friday and Saturday, you'll need to be here no later than 7 p.m. and work until 1 a.m. or until close, which is 4 a.m. Sunday, you must be here at 5 p.m. and off the floor by 10 p.m." She continued, "You're in school, so on Sundays, if you need to leave earlier than 10 p.m., just let me know."

I nodded, taking in the information, and asked if there was anything else I needed to know.

"Yes, there's more." She looked over at Monica with a smile. "I like her. She asks questions."

Monica smiled and said, "That's my girl!"

"Love, you'll need to pay a house fee every time you come to work. If you don't have it when you check-in, then you can pay it at the end of the night. If you don't make it by the end of the night, then you can try again the next day, but it'll double, so always have your house fee."

"But what is a house fee?" I asked with a confused look on my face.

"Duh! I forgot you don't know the lingo. A house fee is a fee a dancer pays to work at the club. Dancers are considered independent contractors, so the house fee is the fee to 'rent' the space for the night and, in this case, be able to use the strip club as your place of business."

She continued going over all the things I'd need to know before starting the following weekend. She gave me a tour of the matchbox club and told me which bathroom to use and how to check into work. It all sounded like I was in a Charlie Brown cartoon. I took the paperwork and read it over that weekend. I had to figure out a way to get a Sheriff's Card. This card permitted me to work in an adult setting and registered me as an Entertainer. Given that I didn't have to be in school until 3rd period, 11 a.m., I went on Monday morning.

I was afraid to tell Rodney about my new job, given his possessive and aggressive nature. But having already lied to him about the baby, I didn't feel very comfortable lying to him again. So, I told him the truth, and thankfully, perhaps due to my tearful puppy face, he didn't blast out like I expected him to. Strangely, he appeared supportive and quite all right with my new job.

Maybe he really does understand our, or at least my, situation well.

The following weekend came, and I showed up early to the club as the lady had advised so I could finish my paperwork.

"All right, Naomi here's the dressing room, and you can choose your locker. Did you remember to bring your own lock?" the lady asked.

"Yes, I got it. Thanks!"

"Okay, go and get ready, and I'll give you the official tour once you're done."

I nodded and began getting ready. Monica had given me a couple of outfits the weekend before, so I could have an idea of what to wear and buy once I got going in the "game." The game was what they called it. It was a stripper's code word whenever "others" were around. "Others" are the normal people who turn their noses up at strippers. Monica also let me borrow her beginner stripper heels that were higher than usual but very comfortable. They were black 7-inch heels, including the platform. They were strappy and held my ankles in place. Monica hooked me up!

65

"Hey, baby girl, you're new here? What's your name?" a skinny, blond-haired chick asked.

"My name is Naomi."

"Aww, baby girl, not your real name," she chuckled. I was puzzled, and embarrassment seeped into my face.

"You need a stripper name," she said. "You can't let your customers know your real name. That's how you get stalked ."

"Stalked?" I yelled out.

Again, with her little chuckle, she explained, "Baby, you never know who you're going to meet in this business. Your stage name will protect your identity. Plus, I heard the boss saying you were still in high school. You don't need that getting back."

"Ooooh, I get it now," I said, nodding.

Maybe I can be Diamond, like in The Players Club. She was in school and dancing.

"What about Diamond?"

"Nah, we have a girl by that name here."

"Hmm, what about Destiny?" I tried again.

"That's a common name in this world too. How about Scarlet?" she suggested.

"Scarlet?"

"Yeah, Scarlet. I know you read *The Scarlet Letter*. You, my dear, have put on the 'Red A.' Though you ain't fucked anyone's husband, you are entering into a world that's very different from what others would consider the 'right' way to make money," she explained to me.

"Well, damn, since you put it like that, I might as well walk around with a red 'S' since I'm a stripper now," I said, laughing.

We chuckled, and that night, Scarlet was born.

Chapter Eight

"Naomi Ann Bowers," the principal announced. I stood up and walked up the stairs to the podium to receive my high school diploma. My family yelled and screamed from the stands. It was a great day. I was officially a grown woman.

Later, at the commencement party, I kept getting asked, "So Nomi, what's next?"

"Well, I'll be starting at the community college for my first two years. I got a scholarship that'll cover my tuition," I'd reply.

"That's right. My baby is smart!" Dad yelled from the background.

Laughing at Dad's remark, I continued, "From there, I'll transfer to the University of Las Vegas (UNLV) to finish up my undergrad and off to my master's program."

"So, what are you going to major in?" my uncle asked.

"Education. I want to be a teacher like my Lola," I exclaimed.

My Lola came over and kissed my head. "I'm so proud of you. I know your grandma Lou would be proud." I nodded and hugged and kissed her back.

My gut got to me towards the end of the celebration as I was running out of steam trying to hide my pregnancy and my night job. Unfortunately, I had to work that night, and people were still at the house, so that meant no relaxing for me.

"Mom," I called out to her and motioned her to come over, "I have to go to work tonight. I'm the only waitress there until 11 p.m. I got to go. Can you tell everyone bye for me, and I love them? They're all over the place, and I'm pushing time."

"Of course, baby. Be sure to say bye to your daddy, though."

"I will."

I said my goodbyes to my parents and friends and left the house in a hurry. I was relieved to have gotten through the day, and as soon as I reached the car, I unzipped my pants and released my belly. My little pouch poked out, and I began to cry. It hurt to keep this secret from my parents, and the secret of my dancing was another burden.

Brushing off my sadness, I called Rodney. "Do you have your money together?" I asked in an annoyed voice. He was still at the house, enjoying my family.

"Almost, why?" he replied.

"Because I can't keep doing this! I'm tired, and I'm starting to show. This isn't just a yolk in me anymore. I can feel the baby flutters," I cried.

"Okay, Nomi, we will go and make the appointment next week," he said.

"Great. I'll see you once I'm off work."

"Love you," he said.

"You too."

***

"Bringing to the stage is our high school graduate. She's smart, sexy, and can hypnotize you with her eyes. Here's to the sexy Scarlet!" the DJ at the club announced.

Suck in and breathe. You got this, Naomi. You got this.

One step at a time, I walked up to the stage covered in red lights. I walked over to the brass pole in the center while checking myself out in the mirrors all around the club. I moved my hips slowly from side to side, finding the rhythm of the music. Pulling my body up, I kicked my left leg and wrapped my body around the pole with my right leg following behind. I pictured myself as a snake coming down from a tree. I showcased myself to all the men sitting around my stage, shaking ever so softly and booty popping to make them go, "Oh yes, baby, yes, Scarlet. You can take all my money!"

I positioned myself in front of one old white man in sweatpants who smelled like mustard. Staring at him with my mesmerizing eyes, I smirked, "Put it here." I opened my G-string to pop the dollars in place on the side of my hip.

"Oh, Scarlet, I like you. Can I get a private dance after this?" The old man leaned in.

I felt a flutter around my stomach. *Private? I don't know if I'm that good yet.* But something stirred inside me, a feeling of being someone else, my alter ego – Scarlet. I wasn't nervous anymore.

"Of course, baby! I'll see you when I get off stage," Scarlet replied in a voice that didn't resonate with Naomi. *Yes, I am Scarlet. No. Scarlet is me.*

After Scarlet's three songs were over, she met the old man in the back of the club by the VIP rooms.

"So, baby, what do you want to do? We can do the 3 dances for $100, but you seem ready for Scarlet, so let's do it big and go for the hour," Scarlet said.

"Oh, honey, I can't do an hour. I got to be leaving soon," the old man replied.

"Okay, 3 for $100 it is, but I'm not getting nude," Scarlet said.

"Now why you gonna do me like that?" the man retorted.

"Because you come in here every week and want the same thing. Only tipping five dollars and then be trying to touch and shit! I don't like that. I need more money, and you have it! I'm getting it today," Scarlet said in a cute yet assertive manner.

Scarlet noticed so much more than Naomi, the shy and introverted girl who could never become Scarlet in reality.

"Okay, honey, I'm sorry," he said.

The old man later became one of Scarlet's regulars, and he was always very easy to convince. He liked her, and Scarlet believed he had a thing for younger women. Nevertheless, he paid well.

"So we're doing 3 for $100, and if you want me nude, I would need another $100. If you want to try to touch me without getting kicked out this week, it'll be another $100." Scarlet was all about business and work. She was demanding and never shied away from outright asking for what she deserved.

"What can I touch?" the old man asked, licking his lips at Scarlet.

"My legs, my shoulders, my back, and my arms," Scarlet replied.

"Can I hug you when we're done while you're nude?"

"Sure, but that'll be an extra $50," Scarlet exclaimed.

"Deal, $350." The old man paid up, and Scarlet began.

"Scarlet, you're gonna give my old ass a heart attack. You take all my money and leave me with blue balls," the old man expressed.

In a sexy whisper into the man's ear, Scarlet said, "But you like it."

Turning around, she swayed her body back and forth and dropped down on her knees in between the old man's legs to do a headstand. She clicked her heels, and the dance was over.

"Thank you, honey!" Scarlet said with a sexy smirk.

"Oh, Scarlet, you are good at what you do. I'll see you next week," the old man said.

"Great, honey, see you next week," Scarlet replied.

***

Owing to my previous talents and dance lessons, dancing came easy to me, and as my game progressed, taking men's money came even easier to Scarlet. And I was desperate. I needed over $2,000 for my half of the abortion cost. I had no idea where Rodney would get his half, but I had to get the money. I had to make sure I could cover my half and his, just in case. God must have been looking out for me because the next night, I happened to meet Jackson.

He was a mysterious personality. I had seen him in the club before, but he never got any dances, nor did he sit and chat with any of the girls. Instead, he'd tip from time to time and make eye contact with me, but this night Jackson came up to my stage, sat through my performance, and made it rain.

It was a thunderstorm. Money was everywhere. Before I could clean off my stage, he said, "Come holla at me when you got some time."

I nodded and piled the money into two big trash bags.

"Guess we know who he wants," a hating ass stripper at the club said.

"I guess so," Scarlet replied. The hating stripper was known to be conniving and slick. She started fights with everyone. Scarlet usually stayed clear of her, but that night, she broke her silence. She never liked bullies, and she wasn't about to be one of her victims. Scarlet kept all her money on her that night. She didn't go into the dressing room at all. Instead, she went and spoke to Jackson.

"Didn't think I'd get to make your acquaintance, Scarlet. I'm Jackson," he said politely.

Scarlet was surprised at his polite, warm address. She was used to Black guys either being pimps or talking nasty and being rude to the dancers, so she stayed clear of Black men in the club, but Jackson was different. He seemed like a businessman but not in the business of women. He didn't give her any pimp vibes.

Scarlet continued to stare at him while he talked. "I've been coming in here for a minute, and you always walk right past me. Why is that?"

"Well, I don't fuck with Black men in the club. They're all pimps or drug dealers or hood niggas that try to be something they ain't," Scarlet replied honestly.

"I heard that you graduated. Is that true, or is it part of your act?"

"It's true."

"You going to college then?"

"That's the plan. Why so many questions?"

"I'm asking because I came in here a couple weeks ago with my sisters and a few of my homies. They all liked your set and said you spoke very well. I figured there must have been more to you. You're smart and pretty, and you speak well," he explained.

"Thank you, but that's not appeasing me. What is it that you really want?" Scarlet replied, slightly aggressively. She wasn't used to people being nice to her, unlike Naomi.

"Okay, okay, I'll get straight to the point. All I'm saying is this ain't for you, and I'm hoping you do more and get out of this shit," he said.

Nodding, Scarlet replied, "Thanks, but you've been coming in here for a while now and haven't said much to anyone in here, so what's up? Are you going through a breakup, or are you just now feeling comfortable talking to someone? What's up?"

"Well, to be honest, I have a business proposition for you."

"Aw hell nah! You're a pimp! I'm good," Scarlet said, getting up out of her chair.

"No, Scarlet, I'm not a pimp. Please have a seat," he asked.

"I'll stand."

"I'm in a business where lots of money is involved. I've seen how you move in this club. You don't fuck with any of the girls. You show up, change, hit the floor, talk, mingle, dance, do some VIPs, and then you change, and you're out," Jackson said.

"You've been watching me? What the fuck type of creeper shit is this!" Scarlet yelled, throwing her hands up.

"I only come to the club to see potential partners, and when I brought my family in here, and they took to you, I knew you'd be a good fit. Think about it, and I'll be back next week."

After saying that, he grabbed his things and left.

Chapter Nine

"Naomi, dear, you're well into your second trimester," the doctor said. "Both the baby and you are healthy. You still have many options. Are you sure you want to schedule the abortion for next week?"

"Yes," I replied as tears flowed down my cheeks.

The doctor handed me a tissue. "Everything will be all right," he said. "In the meantime, I'd like you to go see a therapist and discuss the feelings you're having right now. If the therapist approves of your mental and emotional state – as in affirms that you're ready to carry through with this procedure – then we will make the appointment."

***

"What does that doctor know? Why are we going to this fancy-ass clinic anyways, Naomi?" Rodney exclaimed. "All he does is make you cry and feel bad about your decision."

He was annoyed that we'd let the pregnancy go on this long.

"I understand what you're saying, but given that I am far along, Rodney, he has to make sure I'm mentally healthy to go through the procedure, as my body has changed a lot since the first month," I explained. "I don't want to slip into depression, and seeing a therapist now can make the transition from being pregnant one moment to not the next a lot easier. She'll probably be able to help not just me, but both of us cope," I continued.

"And why you still working at the club if you ain't making any money? I ain't never heard of a broke stripper before!" Rodney said bluntly.

"Well, I had tickets to pay off that you never paid and said you would. Furthermore, I had bills to pay, as I don't have my parents paying my car insurance or phone bill anymore. Oops, I'm sorry, I'm being a fucking adult, and you're still being a fucking child. Where's all the money you owe me and promised me? I don't fucking see it. So shut the fuck up! After this is all over, I'm done with yo' broke ass! Fuck you!" I retaliated.

He glared at me with an open mouth, possibly shocked at my sudden outburst. I'd stopped fighting with Rodney a long time ago and saw him only as a support system to get through the abortion phase. All feelings for him were long gone, and this appeared to be a blow to Rodney's ego. He stood there, frozen, with a perpetually blank expression while I fumed at him angrily. I got into my car and skirted off. Crying and feeling less than, I called the therapist and made an appointment for the next day.

"Hi, Naomi, I'm Dr. Silva. I'll be guiding you through this process. I understand that you are pregnant and well into your second trimester. Is this correct?"

"Yes," I replied.

"You stated on your form that you just graduated. Congrats! That is exciting. What're your plans for the future?"

"Well, I'm currently enrolled at the community college for the fall semester. I'm majoring in education."

"That's good. What made you want to go into education?"

"My grandmother was in education, and my aunt is a teacher. I always found it interesting how they worked with young people. Plus, they had summers off and got to buy cool teacher stuff for their classrooms."

"Very nice. So, what brings you here?" Dr. Silva asked.

She knows why I'm here. I just need her approval for my doctor at the clinic to believe that I ain't crazy.

"I'm here because I'm very emotional about my decision to have my abortion, especially given that I am so far along. I feel bad, but I can't bring this baby into this world knowing that I'm not settled nor in the position to take care of it. What's eating me up is that my parents have no clue about my pregnancy. And also, my boyfriend is a douche!" I said as the tears poured out. The doctor listened to my rant patiently and then assured me of my feelings. She said they were quite normal.

She said, "Naomi, I believe what is eating you up is the secret that you're keeping from your mom and dad. From what you've expressed and shown, you all seem close."

"We are, but I don't want to break their hearts. I don't want them to see me as a failure. They've worked so hard for me to be in this position – going to school and having all the luxuries I have now. I don't want to let them down, you know?" I cried.

"I understand, but why do you feel that you'd let them down by being pregnant?"

"Because they have high hopes for me. They never went to college, and that's been their dream for me before I was born," I said.

"I understand, Naomi, but telling your parents the truth will make you feel a lot better. Trust me on that. From all that you've told me, it seems that your parents are quite supportive, and if you tell them, I'm sure they will be with you through it all. Plus, you won't have to deal with your boyfriend at all. You see the positive side of it?"

I stared at her for a minute. I could see the point she was making. However, a tiny voice nagged at the back of my mind. *You've let us down, Naomi.* I heard it in both my parents' voices. *No, I can't wipe the sincere image of Naomi from everyone's mind,* Scarlet affirmed in my head. She was the protector.

Dr. Silva was waiting for my answer. She had a calm and composed expression, but her fingers slowly tapped the desk impatiently. I nodded.

"Very good," she said. "Naomi, I want to encourage you to tell your parents about your pregnancy. This will make your final decision easier. Can you try that for me, and we can meet again next month?" Dr. Silva urged.

"Okay, but I have my appointment for the abortion next week," I explained.

"That is fine. You do what you need to, but I am encouraging you to tell your secret to your parents so you will feel better about your decision."

I nodded glumly and left the office. Speaking to Dr. Silva made it easier for me to see the light at the end of the tunnel. But telling my parents wasn't a piece of cake, and considering all my other troubles, I didn't think I could handle being in that predicament anytime soon. So, telling my parents could wait. As for the pregnancy issue at hand, I knew I'd be done and through with it soon.

"Nomi, what did the shrink say? Are you crazy or depressed?" Rodney asked and chuckled condescendingly.

I sighed without looking at him. Nothing he said or did bothered me anymore. His retorts felt like a ticking bomb that would go off with my successful abortion and most of his occasional "words of concern" felt empty.

"No, I'm good actually," I replied, cutting through his laughter. "Thanks. My appointment had to be changed to the 26th rather than next week as the slots are filled. The price will still be the same, but I'll need you to have your half of $4,200 ready, and I need you to stay with me, as it may be a two-day procedure."

"It works out perfectly, as my family will be out of town that week, so we're good," Rodney smiled.

"Alright." I sighed again. *One last time at his place.*

***

Jackson was back in the club like he said he would be, and on my set, he threw more money than before. "Come holla at me when you're done."

I nodded, and after cleaning up my stage with bags full of money, I went over to him. "So you returned. What's up?"

"Did you think about being my partner?" Jackson asked.

"I don't know what a partner does. You didn't go into much detail. Can you explain?" I asked.

This time when speaking with Jackson, Scarlet was on hold. It was Naomi. There was no game to spit to him. We were talking business.

"I'll explain, but it can't be here. Just know those bags will keep coming," he said with a serious face.

Taking a leap of faith, I went against all morals of the club and asked, "Where do you wanna meet? I'm off at 3 a.m. tonight."

He replied, "That's too late, and you gotta get home." He chuckled. "How about we do brunch at The Venetian, Grand Lux? Say 1 p.m.?"

"Oh, great." I breathed a sigh of relief.

"I told you, I'm not a pimp. I have no interest in getting money from women," Jackson grinned.

"Well, sir, I will bid you goodnight. You gotta get out of here, as you have an early brunch meeting tomorrow," I said sarcastically.

"Alright. See you then."

"Hold up, do you need my number?" I asked.

"No," he grinned widely. "You either show up or not. If you don't, then this will be our last encounter."

What in the world is this man into? But whatever it is, I have to keep this to myself. No one can know, not even Rodney's ass. Should I tell Jackson about my pregnancy? Maybe I'll wait to see what his business is and go from there. Yeah, that's it. Hear him out first, then tell him about me.

***

The morning came so quickly. I'd barely slept, and I'd also worked past 3 a.m. the night before. I was nervous about today, as I didn't know what to expect from Jackson. I got up and took my time getting dressed. As I slowly walked to the kitchen, I saw a note from my mom on the counter asking me to pick up some milk and bread. I shook my head and yawned wide. *I guess I won't be having any toast this morning.* I grabbed a cup from the cabinet and added a green tea teabag to it. Pulling out a pot from the cabinet below the stove, I added some water and lit the eye. While I waited for my water to boil, I checked my text messages.

Rodney sent: "Morning baby, are we still going to the mall today for our Jays?"

Jays were Jordans. *Ugh, all this muthafucka cares about is his shoes. How about asking me how I'm doing and feeling? Fucker!*

I didn't respond.

The water began to boil. I took the pot off the eye and poured it into my cup. Next, I checked my emails. Nothing was new. I'd gotten my finalized schedule for the fall semester and the confirmation of payment. I was all set to start in August. Sipping on my tea, I finished checking over my emails and then went to my closet.

What to wear? Business casual seemed like the best option. I chose to wear a good pair of blue boot-cut jeans, a colorful blouse with a side bow around the neck, and a pair of brown boots to bring it all together. *This is it; it doesn't say, "Hey, I'm a stripper, and I want to do business with you."* I prided myself on keeping my nightlife separate from my day life. I didn't want people to know me as Naomi, the stripper; instead, I wanted to be Naomi, the good girl who is about to go to college and make something of herself.

***

I arrived at the Grand Lux at five minutes to 1 p.m. Walking up to the hostess, I asked for Jackson. The host pointed me to the bar, and as I approached it, I could feel my stomach turning and the baby fluttering. The baby flutters had begun to happen more and more as the weeks went on.

Tapping Jackson on the shoulder, I said, "Hey you!"

"Hey, you made it and on time too!" Jackson replied. "Have a seat."

"I can't. I'm not of age yet," I said.

"Oh," he said, looking taken aback but then smiling. "No problem."

He got up and motioned the waiter for a seat elsewhere in the area. "I apologize for that. I assumed you were 21."

"No, I'm 18," I said.

"Well, no drinking for you." He chuckled. "What are you thinking of eating?" he asked, looking at the menu.

"I'm not sure just yet, but I'm super hungry," I said.

"Have you been here before?"

"Yes."

"You fancy," he said, smiling at me.

I looked up at him with a smirk. "I know."

The waiter came over and took our orders.

"You got it. Do y'all want any coffee, juices, or cocktails before I put this order in?" the waiter asked while gesturing to the computer.

"We'll have some coffee," I replied quickly.

Jackson smiled. "So you're one of those girls who needs her coffee in the morning, huh? I guess I'll wait to talk business with you. Don't want you being grumpy on me because you haven't had your coffee yet," he said teasingly.

"Ha, that's funny, but I do enjoy the taste," I said. "What's up?" I asked, cutting to the chase.

"Well, dang, let's jump right in," he yelped.

"Yes, I'd like to know some things before our food comes," I replied.

"Alright," he said, clapping his hands together. "First off, I have a business, and it is growing faster than I expected it to."

"And what is that business?"

"It's best if you don't know. I want to keep you as clean as possible. But what I want you to do is wash my money for me."

"Huh, wash your money? Can't you put it in the washer and clean it?" I rolled my eyes.

"Haaaaaaaaa, aww, baby girl, no, no, no," he chuckled a handsome smile. "When I say 'wash the money,' I do mean clean it, but not in the literal sense – I mean make it legit."

"Oh, so how do I do that? And what business are you in? Because this shit sounds funny."

"I'm a dealer."

"A dealer, like drugs?"

He nodded.

"Cool. I can work with that," I said. "Continue. How would I wash the money then?"

"You know how I came in those last couple times with the money? That money was drug money. I wanted to see how you would act with getting hundreds of dollars thrown at you. You didn't get excited. You stayed professional, and after your set, you never came over right after to give me a hug or any of that stripper game shit. You were about your business."

"But I did come over after my sets because you asked me to," I said.

"Yeah, I had to ask you. You never came on your own. Remember, you don't fuck with the Black guys in the club. I got your attention by throwing hella money and asking for you to come and chat with me."

Scarlet was highly flattered. She'd never thought of herself as the ultimate professional or businesslike, and hearing him talk like that about her made her beam with arrogant excitement. And although the existence of Scarlet was only my backup, I felt proud of her.

"How am I supposed to wash this money?" I asked, putting my thoughts about Scarlet away.

"Do what you been doing."

"What? I'm confused." I raised my eyebrows.

"What do you do with the money when you get off or the next day?" he asked.

"I count it and put it into stacks of a hundred $1 bills or five $20 bills. Then I rubber-band them and go to the bank the next morning or a couple days later. Why does this matter?" I asked, still confused.

"Okay, so you have a bank. Do they ask you questions about where the money is coming from?" he asked.

"No."

"That's good to know."

"Why does that matter?"

"Well, it matters because you aren't raising any red flags. For example, I don't have a job, and I don't use credit cards, so if I started putting hundreds and thousands of dollars into my bank account, it'd look fishy. But you, on the other hand, can say that you work at a strip club."

I nodded.

"Do you have a business license?" he asked.

"No, I don't need one," I said.

"You may want to look into getting one so you can open a business account. This account will allow me to access the funds using the card."

"How much am I getting out of this?" I asked. "Also, with getting a business license comes taxes. How are you going to pay for that?"

Getting a business license meant going legit and going on record that I was a stripper. I didn't want that to follow me.

"I will handle all the taxes on the account, and every time I come in and throw money, it'll be over 5K. You can keep 2K of it. Put the rest in the business account. You'll go to the bank once a week instead of every other day."

The food came, and we continued chatting.

"What if it's 7K or 10K that you throw?" I asked.

"Then we'll discuss your cut, but off the top, you get 2K for every transaction," he replied. "Also, when you go get your pampering done, use the business card. That will keep a money trail for taxes. I'll take care of your pampering needs. That should cover any 'extra' that gets thrown on any 'over the top' nights."

"How will I know the money you've thrown from money thrown by others sitting at my stage? Some stages can be really good, you know," I grinned, raising one eyebrow.

"Oh, you're on it. That's a good question. I know that most of the time, ones are being thrown. Should I throw fives and twenties?" he asked.

"That'll work, but I'll also need you to let me know how much you throw so I don't get our money mixed up."

"Alright, businesswoman. I see you!" Jackson replied, saluting me.

"Who's paying for my business license?" I asked, gobbling up a forkful of eggs.

"I'll do that. Here's $300. This should cover the fee. Once you get the license, go down to your bank and apply for a business account. Take this $3,000 to open that. When they inquire about your line of business, you can say you're an Exotic Dancer or an Entertainer. Use whichever you like or feel comfortable with. This will cover the amounts of money being put in." He handed me the guap of money.

"But why not a stripper?"

"Putting 'Exotic Dancer' or 'Entertainer' is more acceptable, and they'll look at it as a profession versus 'stripper,' which sounds more like 'Oh, she'll do whatever for some money.' Being a stripper in some parts of this country holds a bad name. We don't want that, do we?"

"Oooh, got it. I don't want to be labeled as a 'hoe' or 'stripper hoe.'"

"I wouldn't say all that, but here in Vegas, yeah, they'll assume you're a hoe or a carpet walker," Jackson said.

"Oh no! I don't want that, especially given that I do my taxes at H&R Block. I want to be perceived as professionally as possible," I urged.

"Good. I want that too," Jackson said. "So that's the professional line of business you want to put on the form."

"Sure. I can do the license today and the bank in the morning," I said.

"Cool, so we have a deal?"

"Yes, we have a deal," I said as we shook hands and continued eating. "I do have a dilemma that I need to take care of in the next couple weeks, though. This could affect our program," I expressed to him.

"What's up, baby girl?" he asked, sipping his coffee.

"I'm pregnant, and I'm well into my second trimester, but I'm scheduled for an abortion on the 26th of this month," I said it all in one sentence.

His mouth dropped. "Pregnant?! Where? You don't look like it," he said, wiping his mouth.

I chuckled. "Thanks for that, but it's true. The doctor says I'll need to be on bedrest for two weeks and light-duty work for a month. That means I won't be able to dance, but I'll be able to walk the floor. I'll have to pay an off-stage fee. I don't want them to know about my abortion. I keep my personal life separate from the club," I said.

"I understand and respect that. So, you'll be out for a couple weeks? That's fine. When you do go back to the club, I won't throw money; rather, I'll just get VIPs from you. The plan still works. I'll come into the club in a couple days for our first transaction, and then we'll be off for a couple weeks," he said, planning it all out. "Do you have all the money you need for the abortion? I'm asking because if you're well into your second trimester, either you wanted it and now don't know if you really do OR money is an issue. Which is it?" he asked, sounding concerned.

"The money. My ain't-shit boyfriend – well, I don't know what to call him anymore – hasn't got the means, nor do I think he wants to have the means to help. I began dancing to get the money, but I could never make enough to pay for the abortion because I was on a restricted schedule. Then, bills and life started happening," I explained.

"How much you got now?" he said in a serious tone.

"$3,000," I said. "Most of that came from you these last couple nights."

"How much more do you need? And who's taking care of you after? I ask this because I've been through this with my lady when we were younger."

"I need $1,200 more now. Because they had to move my appointment for this week back," I exclaimed.

"Alright. I'm going to give you $2,000 now. This will cover the rest of it. This is an advance for you. You don't owe me anything. When I come in the club this week, just deposit the entire amount into the account."

"Got it!" I said with a sigh of relief.

"We're business partners now. We gotta look out for one another," he said, smiling.

"Also, before I forget, why haven't you asked my real name?" I asked. "We are going into business together."

"I figured when you were ready to tell me, you would."

"Whatever," I said, rolling my eyes. "My name is Naomi, Naomi Bowers. You'll need to know this for our account."

"Well, since you're getting literal, my name is Jackson, Jackson Thompson."

"Nice to officially meet you, Jackson Thompson," I said, reaching out for a handshake. We laughed and enjoyed the rest of our food. We were in business, and my abortion was paid for.

CHAPTER TEN

Day 1

Dear God,

I know that I am terminating a blessing you gave me, but I know you have more in store for me. Please forgive me as I go through this dark time. Lord, please be with me during this procedure. I pray that you guide the doctor's hands and eyes as he operates on me. I also pray that you bless my unborn baby's soul. Forgive me, Lord. In Jesus's name, Amen. Forgive me, oh Lord.

I repeated this prayer in my head the entire drive over to the clinic that morning.

"Naomi, you okay?" Rodney asked as he turned the corner onto the private drive of the clinic.

Breaking my concentration and prayer, I responded, "What do you think?" I was over Rodney and his trifling ways.

"Well, you haven't said much the whole way here. I'm just checking on you. You know we can always take that money and go shopping," he said, putting the car in park.

I gazed at him and sucked my teeth. "Boy, let's go! It's going to take more than some shoe money or shopping money to raise this child," I said, getting out of the car and slamming my door. Little did Rodney know, I'd paid for the procedure in advance to lock in our date. I didn't trust him anymore.

"Damn, baby, I'm only playing," Rodney said.

"I'm not in the mood for games. I want to focus and stay calm. Can you do that with me? Please," I said to him in an aggravated voice.

As we walked up to the clinic, the sliding glass doors looked so sleek and shiny. As they slid open, we walked through. There was no turning back now.

"Good morning, Naomi. How are you feeling today?" the nurse at the front desk asked.

"Good morning. I'm fine," I replied.

"I need you to fill out these final forms, and you'll be all set," the nurse said, handing me the forms. "Oh, and here's your receipt."

"Thank you," I said kindly.

As we went to take our seats, Rodney helped me finish the paperwork. When he realized that the receipt was there, he asked, "When did you come and pay?"

"I came last week. I didn't want to prolong this anymore as the price went up."

"Shit. I see," he replied. "Baby, I'll get you my half soon as I start working. I promise."

I wished I could believe him, but it was his "promises" that had gotten us to this point. I was 22 weeks. His promises were empty, and

I was done. This abortion was my final straw to leave and be done with him.

"Naomi," the nurse called out from the back door.

"I love you, baby. I'll be right here," Rodney said, hugging me and kissing me as I got up.

"I love you too," I said, the reply coming to my lips like a quick reflex, and I wondered how it had turned into a lie.

***

"Hi, Naomi, I'm Stephanie. I'll be your nurse today and tomorrow."

"Today and tomorrow? I'm confused. I knew it could possibly be two days but it wasn't confirmed when I made my appointment."

"Let's have a seat here, and we can discuss the process while I take your vitals," Nurse Stephanie said as we walked into an examination room. Soft classical music was playing in the background.

Making myself comfortable in the chair, I badgered her with the question again. "This is a two-day procedure? Why?"

"Well, given that you are 22 weeks pregnant, we need to proceed with caution as your body has developed more hormones and has changed a lot since the first trimester," she explained, pricking my finger with a tiny needle.

"How does it work then? What will happen today?" I asked as she took a blood sample from my finger.

"Right now, I'm taking a blood sample to check and see if you're still pregnant. After we get the results, I'll have you go use the restroom because we need your bladder completely empty."

"How long does it take to get the results?"

"About five minutes," she answered and continued to check my vitals. "You're normal," she said, smiling. "I'll be right back with your results."

"God, forgive me," I said out loud once she went out. As I sat in the room alone, I didn't feel lonely. I felt a sense of relief come over me, and in that moment, I knew everything was going to be okay. I nodded to myself as the warm relief washed over me.

"All right, Naomi, we're set. The test is positive. Next, you will go use the bathroom, and the doctor will come in and discuss today's procedure with you," Nurse Stephanie said pleasantly. I felt safe.

"Can I go to the bathroom now?"

"Yes, and I'll go get the doctor."

When I went into the bathroom, an instinct arose inside me, and suddenly, I found myself speaking to my baby. *I'm sorry, baby, but Mommy cannot keep you. God, your true Father, will have you now. I love you.*

This day was the day I prayed and spoke to God the most. My grandma always said, "You'll know when you need to speak to God more, but until then, be sure you pray nightly." When I was a little girl, teasing and asking her who she was always talking to, she'd always reply that she was talking to God or Jesus.

In the bathroom, I breathed deeply and relieved myself. When I walked back into the room, Nurse Stephanie and the doctor were sitting in the chairs next to the desk. I took my seat on the examination table. Flipping through my file, the doctor said, "Hello, Naomi, it's nice to see you again. How are you feeling?"

"I'm okay given the circumstances," I said with a nervous giggle. "Stephanie was telling me that the procedure is for two days now. Can you explain in more detail as to why and what will happen today?"

"Certainly, Naomi. Your procedure will take two days as we don't want to send your body into shock. You're well into your second trimester, so your body has begun to develop more hormones and change for the baby to grow and be delivered," the doctor explained. "Today, we will induce you and put you into early labor. We'll insert about 10 to 12 seaweed strings. These seaweed strings will act as expanders to open your cervix. This will be uncomfortable for you, and you'll feel cramping later today."

"I understand that doctor, but labor? Am I having to push my baby out?" I asked, confused.

"No, Naomi, this will help us to naturally abort the baby. Your body will think it is miscarrying," he said. "Usually, by the time the patients leave, their water has broken, and the process begins. The seaweed strings expand more but block the baby from coming out. This will trick your body into miscarrying. You may feel some rapid movement, then no movement at all. This is normal."

"Oh wow! This is a lot," I said.

"It is a lot. Do you think you need more time, Naomi?"

"No. My mind is made up. Will I be awake for today's procedure?"

"Yes. We'll numb your cervix, so you'll only feel pressure."

"And tomorrow? What do I need to know about tomorrow?" I asked curiously.

"Tomorrow, you'll need to arrive early to the clinic. Be here by 8 a.m. I've also already spoken to your boyfriend about what to expect and what time to be here tomorrow."

"Oh, cool, thank you. We'll be here," I said.

"Tomorrow, you'll check in like you did today, and the same routine will happen once you get to the back. Only tomorrow, you'll be fully sedated and in less pain when you leave. I will give you all those instructions today, so you can read over them, and if you have any questions, we can discuss them in the morning," the doctor explained.

"Right on," I said, nodding. "All right. So what now?" I asked.

"Now, we will begin. I need you to turn and lie down on the examination table," the doctor said as he walked around to the front and motioned for me to move down. "Naomi, move down more. You want to feel like your bottom is going to fall off the table."

Inching down, I got into position. "Very good, thank you," the doctor said. He got up and walked out of the room and returned with two more nurses.

Nurse Stephanie stayed in the room during his brief exit.

"Naomi," said the doctor, "these two nurses are here to help pass me the materials. Nurse Stephanie will stay up there with you to support you. Okay?"

"Okay," I said, nodding and looking down at the doctor as he gestured for the nurse to open my legs and level them onto the stirrups.

"All right, Naomi, I'll be talking you through the process. Think of this as your annual pap smear."

I nodded nervously and took a deep breath. Nurse Stephanie held my hand and smiled down at me. "Just breathe, Naomi. It'll be over soon." She demonstrated breathing in and slowly letting it out. I mimicked her breathing. I began to relax.

In the background, I heard the doctor calling for strings. "String... Another one, please... Two more... Thank you."

I continued to breathe and suddenly, WHOOSH!

I heard water splashing on the ground and felt my bottom getting soaked. *Did I pee?*

"Wow, that was quick," the doctor said in a surprised tone.

"Is everything all right, doctor?" I asked while looking up at Nurse Stephanie and squeezing her hand even more tightly than before.

"Yes, Naomi. That was your water breaking," he said quickly and began speaking to the other nurse helping him. "All right, ladies, we need to move quicker. We still have nine strings to insert."

"Stephanie, will it be okay?" I asked, looking for reassurance.

"Yes," she nodded, "this is a good thing. You won't be in too much pain because the doctor numbed the area. Now, later, as the doctor mentioned, you'll feel discomfort but not too much pain, and you won't have an accident of your water breaking while you're trying to rest. The surprise is over," Nurse Stephanie said, trying to comfort me.

I gave her a nervous smile.

"Naomi, you're almost done. The doctor has one more string," Nurse Stephanie said and began demonstrating her breathing and gestured for me to do the same.

"And done!" the doctor called out. "Let's clean her up and get her on her way." He sounded relieved and happy, and that made me feel relieved and happy too.

"Naomi, be sure to get a lot of rest today and tonight, as you'll begin to feel discomfort later on in the evening. If you begin to run a fever, call me. My number is on the paperwork. I've advised your boyfriend to do the same as well. And what time do you need to be here in the morning?" the doctor asked, leaning in with his right ear toward me.

I nodded and said, "8 a.m. sharp."

"Thatta girl. Get some rest and see you tomorrow morning," the doctor said and left the room.

"Thank you, Stephanie, for today and for guiding me," I said.

"Of course, Naomi. You're so brave. It was my pleasure. See you tomorrow," Nurse Stephanie said as she helped me off the table and walked me to the front door and back into the waiting room.

Rodney was sitting nervously in the waiting room. As I approached him, he looked up with a sigh of relief. "The doctor told me that it's a two-day procedure, and we need to be here at 8 a.m. tomorrow," Rodney said, getting up to hug me and walking me out of the clinic.

"Yeah, he said he spoke with you. Do you have the papers? We got to read them tonight," I said.

"I put them in your purse," Rodney replied. "Also, you can only have soup, and your last meal has to be at 7 p.m. tonight."

I nodded. "Thank you."

"I got you, baby. Lie back. We'll be home soon," Rodney said as he drove us home.

***

"Oooooooo," I yelled, waking up from my nap.

Rodney ran in from the living room. "What's wrong? I just checked on you, baby, you okay? You didn't have a fever. What's wrong?" Rodney asked in a panic.

"It hurts," I cried. Tears began running down my face. "Rodney, this is it. That's it. The baby is no more," I wailed.

"Aww, baby, it's going to be okay. Remember, it was for the best. It's going to be fine," Rodney said while consoling me in his arms.

"There's no movement anymore. I dozed off counting the movements. There's nothing," I sobbed. Rodney continued to hold me and rocked me back to sleep. He woke me when it was time for my last meal. I couldn't eat anything after the procedure. I had no appetite.

"Baby, baby, wake up. You gotta try eating something," Rodney said, rubbing my leg gently to wake me. He laid the bowl of soup down on the nightstand next to the bed and pulled me up so I could sit up in the bed. Grabbing a pillow from the other side of me, he positioned it behind my back.

"Baby, I can feed you if you want me to," Rodney said.

"I'm alright. I can do it," I said, lifting myself to a more comfortable position. My pelvis was sore, and I had what felt like the worst period cramps ever. I ate and expressed to Rodney how grateful I was for him being there for me. "Thank you, baby, for helping me."

"Of course, you ain't gotta thank me. I got you," Rodney said, leaning in to kiss me on the forehead. "Eat up so we can get some rest. We have an early start in the morning." I nodded and ate my soup. If only I could trust his promises – but too bad, I was beyond that point.

Before closing my eyes, I whispered a prayer.

Dear God,

Thank you for being with me today. I ask that you be with me while I rest tonight, and if it is in your will, wake me with your morning light. Amen.

Day 2

On my way to the clinic on the second day, I prayed again in my head and calmed my mind and fears.

Dear God,

Thank you for yesterday. Please be with me today. Forgive me, Lord. In Your holy name, Amen.

My grandma had been right. When you need God the most, you talk to Him more. I felt safe walking back into the clinic that morning. Rodney didn't say much on the ride over. He'd held me close the night before. He was on it. It was times like those that made me think we could work, but I knew he was only doing this to save himself. He was no good, and we were toxic for one another. I knew as soon as I was back to being 100% myself, he'd be with the shit again.

"Early morning to you both," the nurse at the front desk said.

"Good morning," we said in unison dully.

"Nurse Stephanie will be out to get you in one moment, Naomi," said the front desk nurse.

"Dang, they just know what's up, huh?" Rodney said.

"Hell, we're the only ones in here. Shit, I'd hope so," I replied with a chuckle.

"Baby, I want you to know that I'm here, and just because we made this decision doesn't mean that I want us to be over. I want us," Rodney said.

"Rodney, not now, baby," I replied, kissing him.

"Naomi, we're ready for you," Nurse Stephanie called out to me from the back of the clinic.

"Hi, Stephanie. How are you?" I asked.

"I'm doing well. How are you this morning?"

"I'm in pain. I've been cramping since last night. But these cramps hurt like hell."

Nurse Stephanie chuckled, "You are technically in labor, so that's a good thing."

"I don't feel any movement," I said sadly.

"That's to be expected," she said, sitting me down in the examination room and taking my vitals. "I know that last night may have been tough for you, but you will get through this," she encouraged me.

"Thank you for that. I'm ready," I said.

"Now, there is one last thing, Naomi," Nurse Stephanie said hesitantly.

"What?" I asked.

"The doctor has one last paper for you to sign. It is giving him consent to tell you the sex of the baby. You have the option to know. We usually don't reveal the sex of the baby to the patient, but considering how far along you are, we have to ask you and have you sign off on whether you'd like to know or not," Nurse Stephanie explained.

"No. No, I don't want to know. It's over. Where's the paper?" I barked.

Why in the fuck didn't they say this shit yesterday! I breathed. *Stay calm, Naomi, breathe. It will be okay. It is protocol.*

"All right, let me go get the doctor," Nurse Stephanie said, quickly leaving the room.

The door opened and the doctor came in. "Naomi, I see Stephanie has told you about the final paperwork. I understand that you may be feeling upset, but this is protocol, as sometimes having a patient know the sex before the procedure can cause emotions to run high and sometimes even fatal accidents."

"Doctor, it's whatever at this point. Day 1 has happened already. There's no turning back now," I said in an unbothered tone. "Give me the paper. I do not want to know. Thank you for the option."

I quickly signed the paper.

We walked down the hall to another examination room, but this room was dimly lit, with scenic pictures of ocean views on the walls. This room still had the soft classical music playing and smelled of eucalyptus and mint. The examination table appeared to be a mechanical chair.

"All right, Naomi, I see you wore a loose dress. That is good, as you won't need to change," Nurse Stephanie said.

"Yeah, I followed the instructions you provided yesterday," I said, smiling.

"I see, right on!" Nurse Stephanie said as she walked me over to the mechanical chair. "Now Naomi, I need you to sit here. Scoot all the way back. This may feel weird as the back of the chair is slanted forward a little bit."

I scooted back until my body grazed the back of the chair. "Stephanie, this hurts my pelvis," I complained.

"I understand it's uncomfortable, but the chair moves. It will put you into the correct position for the doctor to do the final procedure."

I nodded.

The doctor walked in with the two nurses from the day before, another doctor who was wearing glasses and holding a tray of needles and medicines, and a nun.

What in the world is this nun doing here?

The doctor said, "Naomi, you remember the two nurses from yesterday. They'll be with us again this morning. This is Dr. Neil. He'll be your anesthesiologist today," he said, and I nodded and waved at them.

"This is Sister Nancy. She will be here to pray for us through this procedure. Are you okay with her being in here?" he asked.

I nodded and smiled. "Yes, that is fine. I've been in prayer all day and night, so a little more help would be great. Thank you, Sister," I said, feeling relieved.

"All right, we will begin," the doctor said.

I nodded.

"Naomi, I need you to sit still for me as I'm going to move the chair back."

"I'm holding on," I joked nervously. As the chair began to move, Dr. Neil stepped forward and placed a clamp on my right hand's middle finger.

"This is to track your pulse and blood pressure, dear," he said softly.

I nodded and said, "Okay."

"As the doctor is preparing you, I'll be here preparing your anesthetics. Your form said you aren't allergic to any medicines. That is good, hun," he said. "Your sedation today will not be very strong, as the procedure is short. Think of it as... taking a nap." He smiled and wrapped a pretty purple rubber band around my arm, right above my elbow. "You're going to feel a little pinch," Dr. Neil said.

I closed my eyes, and in went the butterfly-looking needle into my arm. "Aww, hun, see? That wasn't hard," he said. "Just one more drop of medicine and you're done."

I looked up at him and smiled as he bandaged my inner arm up. "Now, I'll do your IV on your hand so you stay hydrated, dear."

Nurse Stephanie rubbed my shoulders and gestured a thumbs up to me.

"All right, Naomi, you're all set," Dr. Neil said holding a mask over my nose and mouth. "Can you breathe in for me through this mask? Relaxing breaths, dear. That's it."

Slowly, with every breath, I began to fade away. The soft classical music played ever so softly. The ceiling transitioned from light blue hues to darkness.

***

"Naomi, dear. Wake up. You did well."

I woke to Dr. Neil's soft voice. He was adjusting warm blankets around me. My body was shaking, and I was freezing.

"Doc...tor, I'm co...." I said, shivering.

"I know, hun, that's the anesthesia wearing off. You're fine. These warm blankets will help," Dr. Neil said.

Nurse Stephanie came over and smiled. "Naomi, you did well. I need you to walk with me. You have to use the bathroom if you want to go home now."

Using all the strength I could muster up, I got up out of my chair and hobbled to the bathroom with Nurse Stephanie supporting me. I plopped down on the toilet, realizing I didn't have my panties on, but rather a diaper with Velcro sides that Nurse Stephanie undid for me. I looked up at her with a sense of disbelief.

"Nurse, is this a diaper?" I asked groggily.

She smiled. "Yes, Naomi, it is a diaper. It's to make it easy for you the first couple days and nights at home, as you won't be doing much walking except to the bathroom."

"Oh," I nodded, fading out.

"Naomi, you gotta try peeing, sweetie," Nurse Stephanie urged as she rubbed my back, and I gained consciousness again.

"Okay, here I go," I said, trying.

After 10 minutes of fading in and out of consciousness, I finally peed.

Drip, drip, drip, psssssssst!

The urine hit the toilet, and Nurse Stephanie cheered me on, "That's it, Naomi. You're going pee. Are you done?" she asked, rubbing my back again to wake me up.

"Yes, I'm done," I said.

Helping me up, she walked me to a back door where Rodney had pulled up the car. Nurse Stephanie walked me out to the car and helped get me into the front seat.

"Naomi, you're safe and you're going home now. Your boyfriend will take care of you from here. Call us if you have any questions," Nurse Stephanie said and slowly closed the door.

Rodney nervously ran around the car to hop into the driver's side. He kissed me, and I faded out again.

When I woke up, it was the next day, and I felt sore and empty. My stomach was flat. My breasts were hard as rocks and leaking. They'd begun to lactate weeks before the procedure, but I'd expected it to stop after the procedure. I read the "What to Expect After the Procedure" pamphlet. It would take time for my body to adjust to not being pregnant anymore.

The final procedure had seemed like a minute, but it was a few hours later. What took 22 weeks to create was gone in a matter of two days. My heart squeezed like a sponge, and I cried.

"Lord, please forgive me for what I have done," I wept.

Rodney rushed into the room. "Babe, are you okay? I heard you screaming."

I looked at him with my eyes full of tears. "I wasn't screaming." I cried.

"Babe, I don't know what you heard, but it was screaming. But it will be all right soon. I'm making you some breakfast," he said. I wiped my face and nodded.

Did I scream?

I was in a daze. I slept almost the entire first week after the procedure, and for the short hours that I was awake, I didn't feel like doing anything.

On Day 7, Rodney took me home. We made sure that Mom was at work, as I was still pretty weak. Mom knew that my period would have me out for a couple days, so it didn't look suspicious that I was in bed all day. The doctor advised I get as much rest as I could the first week, as I'd have my checkup appointment in two weeks.

"Nomi, how was your trip with Rodney and his family?" Mom asked, coming into my room to be nosy and letting the aroma of food seep into my room.

"It was good, Mom. We only went to Laughlin," I said.

"Oh. That's good. It was quiet here without you." She kissed me on the cheek.

"Aww, Mom, I missed you too," I replied, hugging her. "What are you cooking?"

"One of your favorites, chicken and dumplings," she replied. "It'll be ready in a few minutes. Get up and come get a bowl."

"Alright," I said, kicking my covers off.

***

It had been two weeks since my procedure, and I was feeling slightly normal. The bleeding had reduced, but my breasts were growing hard. I expressed my concerns to the doctor when I went for my two-week checkup.

"Well, Naomi, this is normal, as your body was preparing for birth. It will take a couple more weeks for your body to adjust back to normal. In the meantime, I suggest you use cabbage in your bras and use a natural cotton breast pad to catch the leakage. The cabbage will help with the knots in your breasts," said the doctor.

"Okay, I will do that. Also, do you suggest I wear a bra with an underwire? Because I've found that wearing a sports bra is a lot comfier than a regular bra," I said.

"If you find that a sports bra is most comfortable, then stick to that. Listen to your body."

"So, this is it… I don't have to come back for any more checkups?" I asked.

"Well, not so fast, Naomi," the doctor said, smiling. "You will need to come back for your three-month checkup, and that should be your last appointment with us. This appointment is your post-op appointment. We want to make sure your body adjusts itself back to normal completely. So, I'll see you in three months."

***

The day had finally come, and I couldn't hold it in anymore. I couldn't hide the truth from my mom any longer. The guilt was rising with each day, and I realized I had to confess. I couldn't sleep at night, and whenever she inquired about my health, I felt a pang of guilt riding high on my emotions. But the mere thought of revealing the truth to her gave me anxiety. I knew it would break her heart. *Naomi, be strong. You can do this.*

Walking into the bathroom as Mom did her makeup, I said, "Mom, I gotta tell you something."

"What, you're pregnant?" Mom chuckled, not looking at me. Her joke slashed at my confidence, and my heartbeat throbbed faster than bullets.

"Umm… not exactly." I wished my voice was slightly normal, but it came out all nervous and afraid. Mom looked up at the mirror in front of her and caught my reflection. Her smile was gone. Instead, a concerned, worried expression masked her face.

"Did you and Rodney break up?" she guessed, her voice desperately trying to hide her worry.

"No," I said, and she turned around to look directly into my eyes.

"I'm sorry." My voice cracked. "Mom, I did something terrible and made some decisions without involving you."

I began to cry uncontrollably. She rushed forward, putting an arm around me. "What's the matter, Nomi?"

I opened my mouth to say, but only a gurgle escaped my lips. I continued to sob and buried my face in my hands. *This is worse than I imagined.*

Mom patted my back and pulled me into a hug. "Now, Nomi, stop crying and tell me, what is it? I'm here for you."

I looked up and sniffed. She brushed off my tears and led me to her bed. We sat at the edge, and Mom took my palm into her own. "What is it, Naomi?"

Her voice was magnetic. A magical warmth flooded through my veins, and my heartbeat slowed down to its regular pace. I took a deep breath, and the words tumbled out of my mouth.

"Mom, I got pregnant in high school. I had my abortion two months ago," I said quickly, anxious to blurt it out before she could react. "I was 22 weeks, Mom. I was shit scared and frightened to tell you. Rodney and I didn't tell anyone. I didn't want to make you mad, or worse, feel disappointed in me for being that 'pregnant high school daughter.'"

Her face was expressionless, as though she were making a conscious effort not to react in any way that would intimidate me, but after she'd searched my eyes for a few seconds, her features softened and her eyes turned moist. "Oh, Nomi...."

"I know! I'm the worst daughter ever," I cried.

"No, you silly girl," she rebuked me, although tears were already pouring down her face. "I'm just mad that you didn't tell me. Did you really think I would be mad or disappointed in you? Don't you know your parents at all?"

I stopped crying and gazed into her tearful eyes. I saw the compassion etched in them before she pulled me into a loving embrace.

"You're mine, Nomi," she whispered in my ear, "and I will always be proud of you, no matter what. We make mistakes, but you shouldn't have had to go through that alone. We would have figured it out regardless if you wanted to keep it or not. We would've figured it out. My baby, it is okay. I'm happy you told me now, at least." She kissed my cheek and I straightened up, wiping my face.

"I'm sorry, Mom, for keeping such a huge secret from you," I said.

"It's all right. I can understand why you did it, but baby, you have to understand that I will always love you regardless of your decisions. You make Mommy proud every day. Even when I'm disappointed, I am still grateful that you're my daughter, and I have to understand that you're grown, and you have to go through some things to learn," she said. "My mom always said I'd learn when I had my own child that regardless of what they do, you will always love them and want to protect them, but sometimes it's not always possible. I understand her words now."

Nodding, I rested my head on Mom's shoulder and closed my eyes, a few tiny droplets still hanging from my eyelids.

"It's okay, baby, we will get through this part together," Mom said. "But please, baby, please let Mommy know whenever you're going through a tough time. Do not be afraid to tell me anything. You're mine, and I love you."

She walked me into my room, helped me get into bed, and tucked the blankets around me, reminding me of when I was a little girl. I smiled weakly at her.

"Get some rest now. I can tell you didn't get enough sleep." She returned my smile.

"Alright. Thanks, Mom. I love you," I said.

"I love you too, and you're going to be fine. I'll see you when I get off."

CHAPTER ELEVEN

By the fall semester, I was cleared by the doctor to resume my normal activities. I was still working at the club and paying my off-stage fee. Finally, a few weeks after the abortion, I garnered the courage to break up with Rodney, as planned, once and for all. He did throw a bit of a tantrum at first, but when I didn't budge from my decision, he snorted and left. Perhaps he thought I would return someday. Little did he know that I'd been done with him long ago.

With Rodney out of the picture and my body reverting to its original state, life was good. My parents still didn't know that I danced, and I kept it that way. I found it easier to say I was cocktailing at night and schooling during the day – until, one day, Mom's best friend asked if I wanted to work at the Hilton.

"Nomi, I know you're in school and all, but have you thought about working and starting a career somewhere while you complete your degree?" she asked.

"No, I work at night, and that pays my mini bills," I said.

"Well, the Hilton is hiring. I think it'll look good on your resume for when you graduate and decide to enter the workforce."

"I don't know. My degree is in education, and I ain't trying to clean rooms. I'm unsure how that'll help me."

"Girl, I didn't say anything about cleaning rooms. I know that's not for you," she smiled. "The Hilton is everywhere and they're corporate. You can teach and train with them if you decide the classroom isn't for you. Think about it. It's good to be versatile," she urged and winked at me.

"I guess I'll look into it. Thank you for the plug," I said.

I valued her opinion and insight, as she had gone to college and worked her way up to VP at the Hilton and her life was pretty nice. I went onto the Hilton's website and checked out their openings. They were hiring for Front Desk.

Hmm, I can do that. I always worked in an office for my summer jobs in high school. How hard could it be? Maybe Mom's BFF is right. I could do a lot with the Hilton while I'm in school, and that'll take me out of the club.

I submitted my application. I called Mom's friend to let her know I had submitted my application online, and she was ecstatic!

"Okay, Nomi, girlllll, you are on your way. I'm happy you thought it over. It's always good to have different skills in your toolbox when it comes to working and building a career."

"Thank you for the pep talk. I appreciate it a lot." I said gratefully.

***

Before I knew it, I was working at the front desk at the Hilton. I had a plan. I went to school during the day, I worked the graveyard shift at the Hilton, and on my off days, I worked the club. I was making money and doing everything I wanted to do. I was almost independent.

"Dad, I'm thinking about leaving the nest, but I'm not sure how Mom would take that," I explained to Dad over lunch.

"Well, baby, you're in college now and doing pretty well. You have a good job. Do you think you're ready?" Dad asked.

"Yeah, I know I'll have bills, but I've been paying my car insurance and cell phone bill for a while now. How hard could it be? I've been with Mom almost every time she went to pay for power or cable. I know how to do that."

"I see, so you have an idea," Dad said, leaning back in his chair. "All right, baby, now Daddy is going to talk to you as an adult." He gazed at me. "If you can figure out your budget, how much you make every two weeks after tax and deduct the bills you have now, we can figure out if you can move out on your own and be successful as an "Independent Woman," as Beyoncé would say." He finished with a laugh and started singing, "All the women who are independent...."

I finished the song, "Throw yo hands up at meeeeeeeee!"

"But Dad, that was Destiny's Child," I mentioned with a giggle.

"Beyoncé was in that, so it counts!" Dad replied, laughing and bouncing his head to the imaginary beat. We laughed and agreed that we'd discuss this once I made my budget. I knew Dad meant business because Mom would worry and probably call him to have him talk me out of my decision to move out. We needed a plan so that he could take control of the conversation if that did happen.

***

The fall semester was coming to a close, and I was doing well. I'd managed to keep my grades up while working my full-time job and running my side business, finishing with 15 credits completed. I also got my budget done just in time for the new year.

"Dad, it's done! I got my budget done, and I can afford an apartment that is no more than $750 per month, which leaves me $400 extra to pay my utilities. However, I can only do an electric-only apartment, so I'll have one utility bill," I explained.

Sitting on the couch, Dad said, "And what about cable?"

"I'm not going to have cable, as I work graveyard, and when I am home, I'm sleeping. So it's an unnecessary expense for me," I said. I'd learned about expenses, assets, and liabilities in high school when I took an accounting class as an elective. It had finally paid off.

"That makes sense. So, what's your monthly budget? Is that $400 extra every two weeks, or is that for the month?" he asked.

"It's extra every two weeks, so for the month, I'll have $800 extra," I explained.

"Oh wow! My baby is making good money at the Hilton." Dad was surprised.

I was making really good money at the Hilton. I based my budget off of my checks and not my business at the strip club, as some months were worse than others. Plus, I didn't want Dad learning that I was still working at the club. Once I'd gotten my position at the Hilton, I told both my parents that I wasn't at the club anymore because they were always concerned about the club I so-called "cocktailed" at. I must admit, I didn't blame them because the teen club had many violent shootings going on. I had to always stay up to date with the news just in case they asked me about the teen club. If they only knew.

"Can you help me look for an apartment, Dad?" I asked.

"Yes, baby, Daddy got you, but you gotta tell your mom."

I smiled, rolling my eyes at the same time.

"If you tell her soon, we can have you set up in your new place before you return to school," Dad urged.

"Good thinking, Dad," I said, hugging him tightly.

"All right, well, I got to get ready for this gig tonight. Get home safely. Or are you staying here tonight?" Dad asked.

"Nah, I'm gonna head home. I have to work tonight," I said.

"My working girl! Daddy loves you!" he said, getting up and walking me to the door.

"Love you, Dad, and thank you!"

"Love you too, baby!"

***

That night, I didn't work at the Hilton. I went to the club. It had been a little over a year now that I'd been stripping at the club. It was still small and smelled of bleach, cigarettes, and sweet body mist. I'd learned a lot about the game that year. In the time leading up to my abortion, I'd had to learn to talk to people and get their money without them seeing me on stage. I learned how to talk game to men and get their money. I'd watch and listen to some of the OGs in the club and mimic them. I also had Jackson telling me what men liked and what they thought while sitting in the strip club. I learned more about how to run my business account and use my business license.

A couple girls in the club had their business licenses but never opened a business account. One of the girls I "trusted" would talk about her business license and the endeavors she was taking on. Her name was Cash. Cash was a tall, light-skinned Creole woman that could move her body like a snake on the pole. She was every man's fantasy, and she taught me how to become a better entertainer on stage and file my taxes for my business. We never got involved or discussed our personal lives, as it was kind of a stripper rule not to get too personal with one another. Men talk was fine, but other stuff was touch and go. You never knew who'd be listening, and in the strip club, you can't trust anyone.

"Scarlet, tax season is coming up. Who're you filing with?" Cash asked.

"I don't know. I've always gone to H&R Block," Scarlet said.

"Girl, they charge an arm and a leg, and they don't itemize your stuff. I have a guy I've been using for years, and he specializes in dancer taxes," Cash said. "Use him!"

"Sure, I can try him out. Hell, I ain't got shit to lose," Scarlet said.

"Here's his business card. I'd suggest you write down everything you spend money on when it comes to the club. Write down your gas mileage and everything, girl," Cash suggested.

"Thanks," Scarlet replied.

By the time tax season came around, I was settled into my new place, and the spring semester had started. I was in the routine of living on my own and working. I got some more time to reflect and wonder what I wanted to do with Scarlet. Her job was done; the plan to "get the money and get out" was over, but was I ready to let go of her?

I was doubtful. I'd continued to work at the club for a few more months to get the financial stability, and now that I was settled at my Hilton job too, I was curious about Scarlet's fate. *Are you crazy?* I heard Scarlet's sexy, confident voice. *I am what you'll never be. Plus, I'm your backup, baby.*

Her words resounded in my ears as if she was a real person distinct from me. But she had a point. I enjoyed the luxury of having what my friends couldn't afford. I enjoyed being able to travel for a quick weekend, and I wanted to step up my traveling game. Traveling to different countries takes loads of money, and I knew how to make it and get it. I didn't want to be broke. I had to get money. And yes, I did agree; Scarlet was what Naomi could never be. So, I continued to work every day, whether it be at the Hilton or the club.

I went to see the tax man Cash suggested. He was a fat, round white man who wore glasses with gold frames and dressed in suits that were way too big for him. Minus his looks, he knew his stuff.

"Naomi, I see that you work and have a business. Are your work and business accounts the same?" the taxman asked.

"No, I have a personal account, and the business account is separate. Why do you ask?" I said.

"I only ask this because, well, off the record… because you dance, you make liquid. Liquid means you make cash-only transactions, and your business license isn't an LLC, so the business account is unnecessary. Also, looking at the account, you only spend about a grand a month, but your account keeps going up. You have to spend more or make a big purchase, so you don't get taxed out of the ass for dancing," the taxman explained.

"Oh wow, I didn't know that. So I don't really need the business account?" I asked to gain clarity.

"No, it is unnecessary. Your work at the Hilton and your dancing can be filed together because your business license allows you to claim only monies that you use. Because your business is all cash-based, you only claim what you 'spend' on," he said, using air quotes on the word "spend."

"Got it. Moving forward, what should I do?" I asked.

"Well, Naomi, we'll file your taxes today to get you filed for the year, and in the next four months, make one big purchase and close out your business account. This gives you one tax quarter to make next year's filing good, and you won't have to pay back a lot of money because right now, you owe the IRS $1,632.52."

"Damn! Okay, I can do that. I can pay the IRS using my business account, right?" I asked.

"Yes," he replied.

"Thank you. I guess I'll see you in four months," I said, getting out of my chair to shake his hand.

***

Jackson needed to know what I'd learned from the taxman. I wondered why he hadn't touched the money. My business account had grown significantly, and there were transactions only from me. So, I called Jackson and arranged a meeting to discuss the issue on his end because now I had to pay the IRS.

"Jackson, we need to meet so we can discuss my taxes – well, our taxes," I said.

"Cool, let's go for a walk and chop it up," Jackson replied.

The next day we met for our walk, and I told him everything and how I was thinking of closing the account.

"You have four months to make a big purchase and close the account so you can file your taxes again on the business?" Jackson asked curiously.

"Yes. The taxman said I don't need a business account for the type of business license I hold. However, we have a deal, but you aren't using the account. What is going on? I have to pay the IRS this year," I said, irritated.

"It's alright. Pay them using the business account," Jackson said.

"Oh, I am, shit," I replied. "But what's going on with you? You've stopped coming into the club every week, and it seems like it's turning into only once a month that you drop in now."

"Well, things have been a little hot on my end, and I don't want to get you looped into any of my problems," Jackson said. "I haven't touched the money in the account because I got rid of the bank card months ago when I got into some trouble with the Feds."

"The Feds? What the fuck!" I yelled.

"Yeah, remember there was a few months you ain't see me? I was locked up. I got rid of the card so they wouldn't think I stole it or that you had anything to do with me," he replied. "I got caught up in a deal that went south, but they couldn't find any evidence linking me to the actual deal, so they had to let me go."

"Oh wow! Well, that doesn't make me feel comfortable at all," I said.

"I understand. We have four months to make moves, then," Jackson said, clapping his hands together and nodding with a smirk.

"Yes, four months, and that's it. What do you want to do?" I asked.

"If my calculations are right, you should have a little over 30 grand in the account. I know the last few months, I've gotten dances worth 9K or more," Jackson smirked.

"That's about right. It's actually a little over 32 grand, as I haven't been needing to get my hair and nails done as much anymore," I replied.

"That's cool. Give me some time to think, and I'll have a plan for you at the end of the week. Thank you, Naomi, for riding with me. I appreciate it a lot," Jackson said.

"Of course. You've helped me out a lot. That $2,000 off top worked!" I said with a giggle.

A week went by, and Jackson called to schedule another meeting. We decided to go to dinner and discuss his plan.

Clapping his hands together and inhaling deeply, Jackson began, "Naomi, we're back where it all started, good ol' Grand Lux. I like this place."

I nodded, sipping my water.

He continued, "But let's get to it, shall we? Since there is $32,000 in the account, some of that belongs to you, as I've come to the club and thrown more than what we agreed upon; every 5K, you get 2K off the top. I've also taken into account that you don't bother me or check on me or anything really. You've stuck to the agreement and stayed professional, and I appreciate that. I also appreciate you telling me about what the tax guy said. That helps me out in the long run. So, I'm saying all of this to say, make your next purchase a car. No more than $15,000, though."

"WHAT? A car! But I don't need a new car. My car works just fine," I said. Blood rushed into my face. *Damn. He must have seen how old my car is and figured I needed a new one.*

"I realize that you don't need it, but it's time for an upgrade. You can go buy another Neon, but I think it's time for you to get something that says 'I'm a grown woman, and I bought this car on my own.'" Jackson smiled.

"Ha! Whatever, but alright. And what about what's left over?" I asked.

"Get a cashier's check made out to this investment company, T.I.C., then send it to this address: PO Box 55, Atlanta, Georgia 30317," Jackson said.

"Oh, okay, check you out! You're making some investments now?" I asked curiously.

"Yeah, I figured with this extra $17,000, I can pay into some stocks and let it grow over time. That'll always be clean money," Jackson explained.

"Right on. I'll have to look into that later. So, I guess this is it, partner," I grinned.

"Yeah, this is it. It's been a good run with you," Jackson replied, reaching across the table to shake my hand. We sat and enjoyed our dinner and our last encounter that night.

A couple months went by, and I began my hunt for a new vehicle. My Neon must have felt it because I started having a lot of car trouble. I managed to keep my car going long enough to trade it in for a new pearl white 2006 Hyundai Sonata. It came with all the warranties and was gas efficient. I felt proud of my purchase because I'd done my homework, and Dad helped me with the negotiations. *Nice doing business with ya, Jackson!*

Chapter Twelve

The spring semester was almost over, and finals were just around the corner. The Hilton was mandating overtime hours for all of their front desk employees. It didn't dawn on me that the Hilton was also the conference mecca of Las Vegas. Come early springtime, bigshot conferences were being held in the hotel, and it seemed that this year was one of the biggest conference years the Hilton had seen, as the number of attendees tripled.

"Next guest," I called out.

Nodding his head, a tall, handsome young man approached my desk. "Hi, I'm sorry I didn't see you all the way down here," he exclaimed.

"It's no worries, sir. Welcome to the Hilton! How's your day going? Last name on the reservation?" I asked and smiled politely.

"Greer, but my day is going well, really well actually. I'm in town for a conference, but I get to see some family too, so it's worth it. And it's all on the company. I'm good!" the handsome man replied with a chuckle.

He was tall with broad shoulders and a low, wavy haircut. His skin looked like chocolate butter, and he had a country accent that I couldn't make out, but most of all, he had a bright and pleasant smile. *Keep it together, Naomi*, I rebuked myself.

"Right on, sir! I'll need an ID and credit card," I said.

"Here you go," he said, handing over his information. He was a country boy from Florida. I had never heard of his city before, but I recognized the state. I met people from all over the world because of my jobs, but he was the first from Florida.

"Well, Mr. Greer, you're all checked in. I saw that you requested a high floor, and I was able to fulfill that request. Enjoy your stay! The elevators are past the candy shop on your left," I explained.

"Thank you, Naomi. Do you work in the mornings all the time?" he asked curiously.

"No, I'm finishing up my shift. I work graveyard, so I'm ready for bed," I said with a little laugh.

"Oh, well, looks like I'll need to pay you a visit tonight. You work tonight?" he asked.

"Yes, I'll be in after 10 p.m. If you find that you need assistance or information on the hotel or your conference, you can always call down to the front desk. Everyone here is super polite," I said.

"Yeahhhhhh, I can wait for you," he grinned flirtatiously and walked away. "Alright, Naomi, this way to the left, right?" he continued, yelling back as he walked off down the hallway.

"Yes, Mr. Greer. Have a good day!" I said, waving him off.

I walked to the back office, and my supervisor, who was an older woman, said, "Naomi, that man was flirting with you, girlllll!"

"Oh goodness, no, he wasn't," I said with a bashful face and continued, "That man was fine, though!" We laughed and counted out my drawer.

***

It had been a couple years now working at the club, and I managed to get into another, more adult-like gentlemen's club. My first club was still good, and I made good money. However, I started to outgrow it. I wanted more money, less work, and, well, a chance to expose myself to a new audience. So, I decided to try out a gentlemen's club.

Gentlemen's clubs usually had the "21 and up" age barrier and offered more money with less stripping. The new club I acquired was a "21 and up" club but was still fully nude. I didn't mind this because I'd already been dancing fully nude in my "18 and up" club. This gentlemen's club offered more clients and luxuries for the girls.

Gentlemen's clubs usually offered a better dressing room with vanities and a house mom. A house mom was usually an elderly woman who took care of the girls. For example, she'd sell hot, healthy, and homey meals or sell different outfits. She was the one you'd go to if you needed some superglue to fix your heels. A house mom was your mother in the club's dressing room.

Although I was underage, the manager made it very clear that working there was a privilege, and he liked that I didn't have much experience in other clubs. Being an exotic dancer in Vegas can take a toll on you if you work at too many clubs. My girls, Monica and Cash, had warned me against that. A lot of managers in the clubs usually preferred to hire girls who weren't juggling too many clubs because then they weren't taking money from the club, they were loyal, and they paid their house fees consistently.

The gentlemen's club was a two-story building and offered many VIP rooms. It had a "mob" feel to it. There were cherry oak wooden beams with a teller behind a window greeting you when you walked into the club. The teller was usually a sexy woman with big fake boobs. She spoke in a sexy voice that enticed men to pay their fee and enter the club. Once inside, dark burgundy carpets flowed down a long hallway leading to the main level and stairs on the left. The club was dark, with bright lights of red, blue, pink, yellow, and white hues strobing around. The stage had a long, lit runway with a brass pole leading up to the club's second story. Gentlemen on the second level could see the dancer on the pole if she wanted to climb up to the top.

The second level was nice; it gave an overview of the entire club and housed the VIP rooms for hour-long dances and more. There weren't any 3 dances for $100 specials happening up there. 3 dances for $100 occurred on the main floor; they didn't have special rooms for these. It was more like a big open area with big red velvet couches that sectioned off the dance area. You had to sell a one-hour dance or champagne room to be on the second level. There were fully stocked bars on the main and second levels.

This club had an in-house DJ, and I wasn't required to bring and pick my music for my dances. The DJ asked your preferred genre of music and that was it. He played all the tunes and chose all the music for you. I had to get used to hearing my name called for the stage, as I wasn't used to that at my other club. The other club had all the dancers' names written on a whiteboard, and we took turns going up on stage. At this new club, I had to pay attention. There were so many girls in the rotation that if I missed my stage, I might not go on again for the next couple of hours. I learned quickly that the stage was the key at this club because it showcased your skills and body. You wanted all the men to see because then they were more willing to spend money.

"Coming to the stage, we have our sexy Scarlet!" the DJ announced, playing "Shut It Down" by Drake.

Scarlet walked down the runway with each beat, swaying her hips from right to left and looking at each man sitting around her stage. She grabbed the pole, reached her right hand up, and walked around the shiny brass pole. She grabbed the pole with her left hand, lifted her body, and wrapped it around the pole, swirling her body down like a snake onto the stage floor. Crawling on the floor and stopping to pop her black G-string, she collected her money.

"Thank you, baby," Scarlet said. She continued to bounce her ass to the beats that the DJ played, mesmerizing men with her deep looks into their eyes. By the time Scarlet got off the stage, she had secured three separate dances. Each of her customers awaited their turn.

"I'll be back for you, baby, but I need my money upfront so I can do that," Scarlet whispered into one man's ear in a sassy yet commanding voice.

"Okay, honey, here you go. Don't take too long with him. I got more for you," the man murmured as Scarlet swayed away with the other gentleman.

Once she finished her dances with her customers, she took a break and walked the floor. She liked being noticed by the men and enjoyed teasing them. She'd smile and walk past them to give them a view of her blingy outfits. She was always in an outfit that looked like money. Her favorite outfit was a two-piece made out of rhinestones and strings holding it all over her body. Her hair was always straightened with added hair extensions to support the length, volume and sweat. The weave would catch the sweat, which didn't curl her natural hair at the roots. Her hair was long and went down to her waist. Her skin was caramel brown and glistened under the red lights. She stood 5'3" in her normal shoes but 5'10" in her 7-inch, open-toed, two-strap stilettos that were mirrored on the outside and black cushioned inside. She walked with confidence and fierceness that demanded money if you wanted her time.

"Excuse me, miss. Don't I know you?" a man mentioned as Scarlet walked past the bar.

She froze. It couldn't be. *But has he recognized me already?* She panicked. *Oh my God, please don't let it be true.*

"Excuse me, what?" Scarlet said, now out of her element and turning to look at the man.

"You look familiar. I know you from somewhere," he continued, but he had a puzzled look on his face.

"Oh, baby, I doubt it. Where you from?" Scarlet asked in the most confident voice she could muster.

"I'm from Florida. I'm here for a conference," he said, and almost immediately, he blurted out, "NAOMI!"

"Hush, Mr. Greer!" I said, gesturing for him to keep it down. "You'll blow my cover. I'm Scarlet here."

"Oh, wow! I'm sorry. I would never have guessed this as a side hustle for you. You look so different and fine, of course, but wowwww!" Mr. Greer said, astonished.

"What side hustle would you think I'd do?" I asked.

"I don't know. Tutor kids? You work at an international hotel," Mr. Greer said.

"Well, can you keep my secret?

"Yes, Nao…I mean, Scarlet. And also, call me Daniel. We aren't in the office," Mr. Greer said, winking at me.

"Thank you. I gotta get back to work. I'll have a drink with you a bit later. Enjoy your time!" I said.

***

Back at the Hilton, Mr. Greer continued his weeklong stay and didn't say a word. He kept his promise. The morning before he checked out, he came by the front desk before I got off and asked, "Will it be all right for me to visit you again? I kept my distance so I wouldn't make you uncomfortable, but I'd like to see you again and possibly enjoy a dance with you?"

"Mr. Greer, I cannot control what you do in your leisure time. You are more than welcome to roam the Vegas streets and clubs," I said, smiling and winking at him. "I'll be there tonight, actually, as tomorrow is my day off," I added.

"Cool. This will be fun. Thank you for allowing me to come," Mr. Greer said.

"Yeah, yeah, yeah. You better come with some money!" I said, using my Scarlet voice. "Now, go to bed. I have to finish out my shift."

Mr. Greer walked away, shouting, "Alright, Naomi, this way to the left, right?"

"Good night – well, morning to you!" I said, waving him off.

***

Later that evening, at the gentlemen's club, Daniel returned like he said he would. He walked in with a smile and asked for me at the teller's desk.

"Scarlet, there's a man here asking for you at the teller's desk. He said he'll be at the bar waiting for you," the house mom said.

This club was good about letting the girls know when they had customers or people asking for them. They all wanted their cut. I learned that if you want people in the club to watch your back or act as if they care, you had to tip them some money for their good deed; they'd take care of you.

"Thanks, Mom! I'll go back out in a few. I need to finish eating," Scarlet said, eating her salad and French bread.

Walking onto the main floor of the club, Scarlet saw Daniel and gave him a shy wave. Getting into her element, she roamed the floor for a bit before giving Daniel any of her time. Daniel watched her as she swayed across the room, making contact with other men. Scarlet could feel Daniel's eyes on her, and she continued to give him a show. As she bent down and whispered in men's ears and cut her eyes up to him, he watched her. Scarlet made her way to Daniel, and his face brightened up.

"Finally, I can get some attention," Daniel said, smiling from ear to ear.

"Yeah, you can't get all my attention," Scarlet said and continued, "What you drinking?"

"I'm having vodka soda right now. Would you like something?" Daniel replied.

"Eww, we need shots. Get us some Patron shots," Scarlet commanded.

"Patron shots it is!" Daniel agreed.

The bartender brought over six Patron shots, and Scarlet and Daniel took three each.

"Oh my! This is going to be a long night," Scarlet said.

"I agree," Daniel said, wiping his mouth and laughing. "So, how did you get into dancing?"

"A dilemma," Scarlet said, trying to stay in character.

"Oh, must have been a big dilemma," Daniel said, nodding his head, rubbing his hands on his knees.

"A little bit, but I like it now. I like having a man's attention and controlling him in a way that I can't explain," Scarlet said, giggling.

Naomi stirred as she heard what Scarlet had just said. *Wasn't the dancing and stripping only a backup?* Looks like that wasn't the only case anymore. I blushed, feeling Scarlet's confidence inside her body. *Hush,* Scarlet told me, and Naomi went back to sleep.

"I can dig it. Can you control me?" Daniel asked, intrigued.

"I'm doing it now. Whatever I tell you to get, you will get it. Your eyes haven't left the sight of me," Scarlet said, raising her right eyebrow and rolling her eyes with a smirk on her face.

"Hmm, you're right. I like what I see. I've been liking it since the very first day I met you, and you checked me in," Daniel exclaimed.

"Whatever!" Scarlet said, rolling her eyes again.

"Should we order more shots?" Daniel asked.

"Sure. I'm down," Scarlet said.

Daniel wasn't like any of the other men in the club. He knew who Scarlet was outside of the club, so I was comfortable talking to him, and soon, Naomi was back up again, although Scarlet wasn't completely out of commission. Naomi talked while Scarlet played.

We talked about everything from birthdays to life and plans for the future.

"So, how are you working here when you are, you know, underage?" Daniel asked curiously.

"I have connections," I said, laughing, "But I got lucky. I auditioned and got hired. It wasn't until I did the paperwork that they found out my age, and they allowed it. I'm on a strict contract that says, don't start no shit!"

"Oh, that's dope. So it's fine for you to drink?" Daniel said, concerned now.

"Yes, it's fine. I know my limit, and I'll be 21 next year. I usually stop drinking by 2 a.m. and start my coffee and water binge to sober up so I can drive home. And if I can't drive home, I call my cousin or a cab," I explained.

"You got it all figured out. That's smart," Daniel said, nodding his head and still smiling from ear to ear.

"Yeah, so what do you do? I know you are here for the tech conference, but what's your job?" I asked.

"I'm the IT guy for my current station. I'm here learning more about which companies can offer better services and technologies for the military," Daniel explained.

"Oh wow! Military boy! I see you," I said, excited and intrigued.

"Yeah, it's pretty cool. I have a few companies that may work for us on my base. This conference was eye-opening and fun," said Daniel.

"Right on. That's good," I said.

"What else do you do, Naomi? Oops, Scarlet. I'm sorry," said Daniel, giggling.

"I work at the Hilton, and I go to school."

"Nice! What are you in school for?"

"Education. I'm studying to become a teacher," I said proudly.

"Whattttt! A teacher, that's dope! I'm talking to the future Miss…?" Daniel said, waiting for my last name.

"Bowers," I replied.

"I'm talking to the future Ms. Bowers!" he said. "I don't think I know any teachers."

"Well, I'm your first then. Nice to meet you, sir," I said jokingly, grabbing his hand and shaking it.

"Well, Scarlet, it's been some time, and I don't want to get you into trouble," he said, dragging his voice out and rolling his eyes and laughing, "but should we do a dance?"

"Oh, whatever," I replied, "but yeah, we can. We can start with the three dances for $100. That's cool?" I asked.

"Let's do it," Daniel replied.

***

Getting up from the bar, Scarlet took Daniel's hand and began leading him down the steps to the "3 for $100" lap dance area. Daniel's hand was sweaty and cold. He followed Scarlet. The lap dance area was tucked away in the back of the club. The room opened up to tall, red velvet horseshoe-like couches that gave a certain privacy to the dance. They entered, and Scarlet gave her name to the bouncer guarding the area.

"Why did we have to check-in?" Daniel asked.

"Because it lets the bouncer know how many dances we're doing, and he also calls the DJ to move my name back in the rotation," Scarlet explained.

"Super technical and organized. I like it!" Daniel said excitedly.

Walking towards the back-left corner, Scarlet led him to their dance area. "All right, Daniel, here we are. This will be our room, couch, or whatever you want to call it for the next three songs. Please let me know if at any time you feel uncomfortable, and I'll end the dance. You are not allowed to touch; however, you are allowed to touch my legs and arms. Do you understand?"

"Yes, I understand," Daniel replied.

The dance began, and Scarlet repositioned Daniel to the middle of the couch. She began standing in front of him, allowing him to see her body move to the music. The DJ must have had an R&B genre girl on stage because he was playing "Touch My Body" by Mariah Carey.

Scarlet's hips moved from right to left in a sensual way. She turned around and bent over, glancing over her left leg to stare at Daniel. Swooping up and rolling back down to the floor, Scarlet got on her knees. She began crawling up to Daniel and in between his legs. She kept her eyes on him, looking deep into his eyes to mesmerize him. He stared at Scarlet lustfully as she used his knees to push her body up, closer, and upward. Rolling her body in a wave motion, Scarlet lifted her left leg and grabbed it to show off her flexibility.

Daniel took his right hand and reached up to touch her leg. He inhaled deeply and said, "Oh my goodness, you are so sexy to me."

Scarlet, in her sassy yet sexy voice, whispered to him, "I know."

She continued to dance for him. T-Pain came on as Song 2, and Scarlet lifted herself onto the couch. She stepped one foot up and then the next so that she was standing above Daniel's face. She removed her top and wrapped it around Daniel's neck.

While bending over, she brushed her boobs over his forehead and straddled him. Daniel was breathing deeply, and Scarlet felt Daniel's dick getting harder. She continued her dance and moved her hips around and up and down. Daniel put his head back.

Scarlet was enjoying making Daniel go crazy. She could only imagine what was going through his mind. She stood up and rolled her pussy in his face and put his head back up to catch a whiff of her scent. But when he put his head up, Scarlet was in the middle of her body roll, and his chin and lips hit her pussy, moving his entire head back.

"Oh, I'm sorry, Daniel, did I hurt you?" Scarlet asked and continued, "I misjudged how close I was to you."

Without a word, Daniel moved his head up, wrapped his muscular arms around Scarlet's upper thighs, and began to blow hot air through her G-string. Trying to control herself, Scarlet pushed his head back, but Daniel's right hand had already grabbed the side of her G-string and moved it to the side. He stretched out his tongue and touched Scarlet's pussy lips.

Scarlet melted on Daniel's face. Before she knew it, she was straddling Daniel's face and moving back and forth on his tongue. Daniel was grabbing Scarlet and pulling her down on his mouth. He reached up with his left hand and begin playing with her right breast.

Losing all control, Scarlet slipped into a euphoric realm. She weakened and slid down Daniel's body. Kissing him, she forgot where she was and began grinding his lap. He pulled out his wallet to grab a condom and slipped it on. Scarlet slid down. Kissing him ever so softly, Scarlet rolled her neck back. She began to moan, but Daniel quickly reminded her to do it softly.

"Ooo, you feel so good," she whispered in his ear. Their bodies were close and moving in a rhythm.

Daniel replied, "You feel so good. Damn! You tasted good too."

By Song 3, Daniel and Scarlet had climaxed and returned to their reality.

"Oh no, what did we do? What if they saw us?" Scarlet panicked, stirring up Naomi.

Oh goodness, what did we do?

"I don't think they saw us. Calm down. Let's just chill here till the end of the song," Daniel exclaimed, trying to stay calm himself and wiping a few sweat beads from his forehead.

"You're going to have to tip the bouncer good in case he did see something. Oh my God! I've never done that before. Why did you do it? I mean, it's obvious I didn't mind, but still," I asked, trying to get dressed without falling to the floor.

I was weak and satisfied. Scarlet was going crazy. Boy, I was beyond the craziness and beyond Scarlet.

"Honestly, I don't know. I was feeling the way you were dancing, and I caught a whiff of your pussy, and I was gone. I'm sorry, I wasn't trying to have sex with you. I just wanted a dance," said Daniel.

"Shoots me and you both. It did feel good, though," I exclaimed, propping Scarlet back up.

"Yeah, it did. Before I leave, can I have your number? I would like for us to stay in contact if that's fine with you," he said.

"That's fine, but don't feel obligated because of what just happened," Scarlet replied.

"Oh, no, I don't. I've been wanting to get your number, but you were always surrounded by your colleagues. Y'all are super professional at the Hilton," Daniel chuckled.

"I suppose," Scarlet said, fixing her two-piece and getting herself together to walk out of the "3 for $100" lap dance area. "Well, you ready? Our dances are done."

She led Daniel out. They held hands, and Daniel's hand wasn't clammy anymore. As they passed the bouncer, Daniel gave him a $100 tip. The bouncer nodded and said, "Right on, thanks, brotha."

Scarlet looked back at the bouncer and smiled.

"See? I took care of it," Daniel said proudly.

"I saw, and thank you," Scarlet replied.

As the night went on, Scarlet and Daniel talked some more, and every time, in the middle of the conversation, he brought up Naomi again. It was getting harder for me to stick to my Scarlet persona, something that I hadn't ever had trouble with. Daniel didn't leave the club until closing and made sure to get my number before leaving.

"Please answer when I call. Remember we did this together," he winked.

I was very apprehensive when giving my number to Daniel. "I'll answer," I said, rolling my eyes like Scarlet and sipping my coffee.

"Alright, we'll chat soon. Be sure to get home safely and text me. I've called your phone already," Daniel insisted.

"Oh wow, you waste no time. You do the same. I gotta go change and get out of here. You literally stayed till they turned the lights on," I said, half blushing, half flushed.

"I don't want to leave you," Daniel explained.

"Well, you have my number, and when you're in town again, let me know. We can link," I replied.

"In the meantime, be sure you answer my calls," he smiled.

"Bye, Daniel," I said, walking him to the exit door.

"Alright, Scarlet, this way to the left, right?" he said mockingly, and we laughed.

Scarlet waved him off. And so did Naomi.

CHAPTER THIRTEEN

The new year was approaching, and I was still working at both the Hilton and the club. I decided not to return to school for the fall semester, as I needed a break, and I didn't know if I wanted to be a teacher anymore. Working in hospitality, I started finding an interest in business and operations. Education became boring and wasn't exciting me anymore.

Given that I had more time on my hands, I worked more in the club. I learned more about my game and how to hook guys to make more money. The soft, innocent, giggly Scarlet only worked for older white men, but the sassy, commanding, "take no shit" attitude worked best with middle-aged men of any color.

After the whole ordeal with Daniel in the "3 for $100" VIP rooms, I kept my distance from Black men. Daniel had gotten the best of me that night. I figured I'd let my guard down because I'd met him outside the club and, well, he'd aroused Naomi, which didn't happen with other customers. Nevertheless, I knew better. I didn't want that title of "stripper hoe" despite meeting him outside the club. If word got out, that'd be my new title; my haters in the club would be telling every customer, "You know that one right there fucks."

In July of 2008, the Hilton took a turn for the worse; they began cutting staff hours for the front desk employees. My days of working a schedule were over. Some weeks, I only worked two days a week and others a full five days. Money was funny, but I had the club to keep myself afloat. Although I was in the club more than I wanted to be, I had to pay my bills, and I didn't want to use my savings to do so. By December of 2008, the Hilton had laid me off with little word on if they'd bring me and others back.

I jumped into survival mode. Scarlet was full-time now, working mostly at the gentlemen's club. The "18 and up" club was fun but didn't have many paying customers.

***

"Coming to the stage, we have our lovely Scarlet!" the DJ announced.

Scarlet walked fiercely down the lit runway to greet customers at the end of the stage. They were mesmerized by her eyes as she wooed them with her pole tricks. Scooting and rolling her body up the brass pole and sliding down with her legs in a V, she dropped down into a split. Money was being thrown from all angles. She enjoyed being rained on. "Making it rain" was the term wannabe ballers used when they'd throw lots of money in the air, and it fell on the stage. Scarlet enjoyed taking their money. She continued her stage set, ending with her sensual move of opening her legs to the biggest spender and allowing him to see her diamond clit ring.

Now that Scarlet was full-time, I had decided to get some sexy piercings that'd look good on stage. Scarlet's clit ring was one of them. This drove the crowd wild, as Scarlet didn't do close-ups of her body when she was fully nude. In her head, this defeated the purpose of the fantasy she was going to sell to her next customer. She only rewarded those who paid her the most on stage with a quick look before she left the stage.

"Alright, ladies, gentlemen, and freaks out there, let's give it up for our sexy, sensual Scarlet," the DJ announced as Scarlet picked up her money, put it into the bucket, and exited the stage.

"Hey, Scarlet, baby, you ever think about traveling?" one of the girls asked in the dressing room as Scarlet was refreshing herself from the stage.

"Not really. I have a cousin who does, but I never had time to travel like that. Why? What's up?" Scarlet answered.

"The club is putting together a tour with our sister clubs in other cities. The manager suggested I ask you to see if you'd be interested."

"Oh wow. That seems like a lot, and I'm flattered, but I'm not ready for a tour," Scarlet said.

"I feel you, baby! It can be a lot your first time traveling for work, but it's fun, and you make hella money," the girl pressed.

"I'm good. When I'm ready, I'll go out on my own," Scarlet said.

"Sure, I'll let them know you're passing on this one."

"Whatever," Scarlet said, unbothered, and finished reapplying her bronzer and lip gloss.

***

That evening I thought about what the girl told Scarlet, and I was intrigued. I knew my cousin Zari danced in Dallas, Texas, and traveled a bit for work, but I always had to work at the Hilton, so it was hard for me to travel and dance. I kept the thought in my mind for some weeks before contacting my cousin to pick her brain.

"Hey, cuzzo, how you doing?" I asked.

"I'm good, and you?" Zari replied.

"I got a question for you, and don't be like, 'Ooooh, bitch, you wanna be big-time now' either!" I said, laughing out loud.

"What's up?" she asked, laughing.

"I've been thinking about traveling for dancing since now I don't have to work at the Hilton. I have some time on my hands. What's your experience been like?" I probed.

"Oh, bitch, that's it? I thought you were fucking one of your baller ass customers!" she replied. "I mean, it's cool and fun but can be tiresome given that it does take a lot of planning and preparation because each state and city require different permits to work in the adult entertainment business."

"Oh wow, but it's exotic dancing. What you mean, adult entertainment business?" I asked.

"Bitch, ain't no kids coming to see you! You're in the adult entertainment business. You being an exotic dancer, stripper, whatever you want to call it, it's an adult industry," she said, yelling on the phone in her Texan accent. We laughed at her unique way of explaining things to me.

"Got it, and whatever, bitch!" I chuckled. "But seriously, I think I'm ready."

"Well, you can come down to Dallas with me first to see how you like it, and then we can plan a full trip in a couple months."

"I'll book my flight."

Off to Dallas I went, and my cousin Zari picked me up and showed me the ropes. This was my first time in the South, and I immediately fell in love with the hospitality and food.

"Now, cuzzo, don't be eating too much because it's easy to put on weight here. It ain't like the West Coast where you got salads and shit everywhere," Zari said.

"Yeah, yeah, yeah. The food is so freaking good, though! You've been treating me to all the good places since I've been here," I replied with gratitude.

"Yeah, I gotta show you around because come Monday, we gotta get your paperwork done at the police station, and we'll go up to the club to complete that too. You brought the application I sent to you, right?" Zari said.

I nodded and said, "Yeah, I got everything I need. Thanks again, cuzzo!"

"Cuzzo, I should be thanking you. It's because of you I got in the game. I just took it by the horns, though. You stayed on the fence because of your schooling and profession at the time, but now, my teacher is here! We 'bout to fuck these clubs up!" she exclaimed gratefully.

Zari used to live in Las Vegas but moved back to her hometown, Dallas, when we graduated high school.

"Oh, girl, please! You asked me some questions, and I gave you the information; that's all. You did it, and you doing it big! I am proud of you," I said.

The club she worked in was similar to my first club in Vegas. I couldn't make out if it was a club or an abandoned building. Zari warned me that the club looked bare and tacky during the day, but at night it was popping. I took her word for it because the building was black as we pulled up to the club. It looked like a black box sitting in the middle of an abandoned parking lot with a giant billboard sign that said, "We Got Whatcha Want."

"Where the hell we at?" I asked, turning to look at Zari before getting out of the car.

"We at my club. Problem?" Zari asked, giving me her blank stare and blinking her eyes quickly at me with her lips perked up.

"Yes, where we at? This shit looks scary as fuck!" I said, getting out the car.

"Girl, I told you this shit hella whack-looking in the daytime. Now come on," she said, moving to the door.

Though the outside looked creepy, the inside screamed money and gentlemen's club. The door opened to white marbled floors with two fountains in the foyer and cashier's area. The cashier's area was behind a gray marble desk with brass bars. Once you left the entryway, two big grayish French doors opened automatically to a carpeted hallway with black and gold patterns leading down into the club. Before the main floor, hallways led off to different VIP rooms. The club was set up like a squarish horseshoe. It was tiered with a top level that held the bar and seating area, a second tier with more seating, and a third tier for the lap dance floor. Lap dances could take place there, and the bottom level was where the stages were. There was a big stage with one small stage in front of what looked like the VIP bottle service table.

Zari leaned in and said, "That's where the ballers sit when they come in. That table doesn't get sold often, but when it does, it's a good fuckin' night." We scoffed and walked into the back office, where I met her manager.

"Hi, Naomi, your cousin has told me a lot about you," the manager said, gesturing for Zari and me to take a seat.

"Hi, and oh, has she now?" I said, smirking at Zari.

"All good things, of course," he said and continued, "So let's get down to it. Zari probably told you about the club, but it is a bit different with out-of-state girls."

"Yeah, she told me," I answered.

"With you being a visitor to the club, your house fee will be $10 more than the rest of the girls, but you have an open schedule. You can come and go as you please. Also, dances are the same. If you do any lap dances on the floor, that's your money to keep. Any VIPs, the club gets 30%. We keep track of that by your check-in card," he explained.

"Check-in card? What is that?" I asked with a puzzled look on my face.

"Soooo, Zari didn't tell you everything," he grinned.

"I guess not," I said with a smile, looking over to my right at Zari, who was sitting with her legs crossed, bouncing her top leg up and down.

"Whatever!" Zari blurted out and smirked.

"It's cool. The check-in card is a little microchip that you can tie on your dancer purse or arm, and you scan it on the machines in the VIP rooms. It's simple."

"Shouldn't be too hard," I said, nodding and taking a look at the microchipped key he handed me.

"All right, well, you're all set. I'll take your paperwork and when you come in, just bring all the information and the work card from the police station," the manager said.

"Thank you," I said, getting up to shake his hand.

"Oh, before you go, what's your stage name? I'll be sure to use it come club hours," said the manager.

"Scarlet. My stage name is Scarlet."

That night, in the club, I was so nervous. I didn't know what to expect. I took a couple of shots of Patron to calm my nerves, which seemed to help while I started getting ready and transforming into Scarlet. My hair was straightened with the added clip-in weave piece to stop my hair from getting curly. My makeup was done naturally with golden hues of bronzer on my cheeks, forehead, nose, and chin. My almond eyes were lined with black eyeliner, and my plump lips were colored red.

The outfit I chose to wear first was a black two-piece with gold accents on the strings that tied around my body. Scarlet was ready.

***

Scarlet walked onto the club's main floor and, being the new girl, all the old girls were staring at her, trying to figure out who she was. Scarlet had her swag on. She walked with confidence and only smirked at some men. Zari was already on the floor and bragging about her cousin in town.

"Scarlet, come here right quick," her cousin said, gesturing for her to come over.

Scarlet made her way over, walking tall with her hips swaying from side to side. "Yes?" Scarlet said, arriving in front of her cousin and a few customers.

"This man's friend right here wants a dance. I told him my cousin is here from Vegas, and she can do it," Zari explained, tapping the man's friend on the chest.

Walking over to the man's friend, Scarlet took a seat in the man's lap and asked, "Is what she telling me true?"

The man replied, "Yes, ma'am. Damn, you're gorgeous!"

Smiling and looking the man in his eye, Scarlet grabbed the man by the hand and walked him to the "3 for $100" VIP rooms. But before entering, Scarlet ran her game. "Now, baby, we are doing 3 for $100, but I think we need more time. Let's do the hour for $500, so we don't have to rush. Does that sound good for you?" she asked him, staring him dead in his eyes.

The man couldn't resist and said, "Okay, baby, whatever you want, but I have to go to the ATM first."

"Well, before we do that, how much do you have? I can get us set up and call the cashier back here. That way, you don't have to move," Scarlet suggested, using her sassy sexy voice.

"I have $200 on me now," the man replied.

"Let's start with the 3 for $100, and I'll have our VIP host right here call for the cashier, and you can take out the $500 for the hour. Cool?" Scarlet inclined her head towards the man, and he nodded frantically.

"Perfect!" Scarlet said, pulling him into a hug.

He melted, sniffing her arm as she pulled away from him and told the VIP host what they were doing. Scarlet led the man into the "3 for $100" room and began dancing to the song that was playing. The man was enjoying every moment.

As she danced, she stayed standing. She knew not to get too close to him because the cashier hadn't come back just yet. Scarlet was always sure to secure her transaction first. She also knew that giving him too much attention could change his mind. She kept her distance. Eventually, the cashier came towards the end of the second song and did a cash advance on the man's card for $700.

Scarlet talked the man into getting that much because he'd need cash for later. Scarlet's game was on fire, and she always made it seem as if she was thinking about the men's pockets, since they still had to go home, but little did they know she was setting them up to take all their money.

"All right, Scarlet, you're all set. I'll take you both to the hour VIP rooms," the cashier said and motioned for the pair to follow her.

"Okay, baby, let's go," Scarlet said. The man followed Scarlet like a rabbit following a carrot on a string. He was happy, and that was good for Scarlet.

I have $600 total on me, and I got to pay out $180 for these dances. I got to get him to tip me $200 to break even.

Scarlet was serious business.

While in the hour VIP room, Scarlet had the man run a tab on his card for drinks. She danced a little but sat and chatted to him topless most of the time. As time drew closer to ending, she got up and danced most of the time away so the man would be happy and not feel cheated out of his hour VIP dance.

"You like it?" Scarlet asked.

"Oh yes, baby, you are doing a wonderful job." He grinned.

"I'm happy you like it. Our time will be ending soon," Scarlet said.

"Oh no, why so quick? And how do you know?"

"Time goes by fast when you're having fun, baby. And I know because of the little monitor I checked in with." Scarlet showed her check-in microchip to the man. "That monitor has gone from green to blue, and when it gets to blue, we only have 10 minutes left."

"Oh wow, that's savvy," the man said.

"Yeah, so would you like more?" Scarlet asked in her sensual voice.

"No. Well, yes, but I can't afford it," the man admitted ashamedly. Scarlet smiled. It was the exact answer she'd wanted and expected because she knew he had $300 left on him in cash.

She went in for the kill.

"That's fine, baby, but I need a tip. We spent a whole hour together, and you didn't tip me, not even once. I thought you liked it." Scarlet pouted her full lips and said it in a sexy whisper.

"Oh. I just didn't know I had to," the man replied.

"Yeah, this money isn't all mine. The club gets its cut," she said, shrugging her shoulders and making a sad face.

"Oh, honey, I didn't know. How much would be a good tip?" he asked.

"$200," Scarlet replied.

"Wow! $200! You play no games." He raised his eyebrows.

"Well, honey, that's why I made you take out more, so you could still leave with money in your pocket," she said, cocking her head to the side and adjusting her breasts back into her top.

"Honey, you got me. You gave me a good time and conversation." The man gave in and handed Scarlet her $200 tip.

Smiling and bouncing her boobs up and down, Scarlet took the money, hugged the man, and whispered in his ear, "Thanks, love. Enjoy the rest of your evening."

And Scarlet walked out of the VIP room with the man still standing there looking dumbfounded.

***

Seeing her cousin walk to the dressing room, Zari, a.k.a. Passion, hurried to meet Scarlet. "Well, damn, bitch!" Passion said, high-fiving Scarlet.

"I mean, I had to get it. He was easy. Waffle House is on me tonight, biiitch," Scarlet said, refreshing herself and laughing loudly.

Dallas may be a good look for me.

The night continued, and Scarlet made some good money. A lot of the men seemed to be regulars in that club, so it was easy for her to use her "out-of-town girl" saying to hook many of them. Passion was proud and hoped Scarlet would want to come back again.

CHAPTER FOURTEEN

Back in Las Vegas, I still hustled. I'd left my first club and never looked back. I was making big money, and the crowd in my first club began to get younger rather than older. I liked old man money. I started a routine where I'd spend three weeks in Dallas and a month at home. This was my life, and it made doing my taxes very easy as I had receipts for everything I did, and I built a relationship with everyone who serviced me. My waxing lady, my travel agent, my taxman, my nail lady, my exotic clothing store owner – we all had a good working relationship. They made sure I had receipts for everything, and my taxman took care of the rest. I was an entire business; Scarlet was my business.

A few years passed, and I was in it. The game was me. I had traveled from Vegas to Dallas, New Orleans, Miami, and Puerto Rico. I was known as "Scarlet from Las Vegas" at many of the gentlemen's clubs I frequented. Although I liked Miami, I had to start keeping my distance from there. I always found myself in a position where I couldn't say no, and I didn't mind.

Daniel lived near Miami and would come out and visit me if I was in town. Over the years, we kept in touch and developed a deep friendship. He and I were like each other's kryptonite. We couldn't go days without speaking on the phone or months without seeing one another. When he found out that I was traveling to Miami for work, he made it his mission to always see me while I was there. One time I was there, Daniel expressed he'd be moving to Las Vegas for work, and though I was overjoyed, my heart sank because I found myself falling for him, and I knew that in my line of work, I had to keep my distance. My business came first.

I hadn't been serious with anyone since Rodney, so I was guarded. Daniel was the total package. He was successful, ambitious, smart, kind, caring, and had no kids. He knew what he wanted, and that was me. Only I couldn't be that for him. I had a feeling he liked Naomi more than Scarlet – not that he didn't look at me that way, but because I could be naturally true to myself when I was with him. I never had to control Naomi or Scarlet in front of him; he got the best of both, and I wondered if that's who I really was. Owning up to Scarlet was hard, but I knew I had her in me, and there was no turning around. Eventually, Daniel did move to Las Vegas, and we remained good friends.

Dallas was one of my favorite places to dance because I had my cousin but also loyal customers. Dallas was my cash cow. I knew on average that every night I'd be making $800 to $1,000. This money would go towards my tuition if and when I decided to go back to school. That was one way I would satisfy myself when I justified this life.

Dallas taught me how to work the pole. My pole tricks had been decent, but in Dallas, I learned to walk on the ceiling and dance with a partner. I never did two-girl shows because I never liked the idea of sharing my money, but there was this one girl, Carmen, in Dallas who asked me, and I agreed. She was a beautiful woman and had been at this club for a while. She was known as the top moneymaker in the club, so it was beneficial for me.

"Hey, love, I need a partner for this stage set. You want to do it with me?" Carmen asked.

"I'm down, but you know I don't dance like you," Scarlet replied. Carmen was a southern dancer. She did pole tricks, flips, and all types of treats. Scarlet did sensual moves and pole.

"Yeah, I know, I'm having the DJ do a sexy set, and you'll be perfect for it," she explained.

Carmen was a thick redbone woman who had curves for days. I'd never looked at a woman before, but she was bad!

"Bet! Let's make it happen," Scarlet said.

Passion peeked her head around the corner, smiling. "So, bitch, you got Carmen after you?"

"What? It's just a stage set. She makes money, and she can see I do too. It makes sense," Scarlet replied.

"No, Nomi, Carmen doesn't dance with just anyone. She only dances with chicks she likes. She's bi," Passion explained.

"Oooooooo, I get it now. Well, this is business," Scarlet explained, getting up to make her way to the stage.

Indeed, she felt nervous, but knowing why Carmen might have picked her, Scarlet's kinky insides were melting.

Am I attractive to women too? Scarlet threw her head back and laughed.

"Ay, y'all, I got a special set coming up for y'all. We got sexy, sensual meets down and freaky! Coming to the stage y'all, is double trouble, Scarlet and Carmen!" the DJ announced.

Carmen walked on stage with a whip in her hand, dressed in all black, and Scarlet crawled onto the front of the stage in her all-rhinestone outfit. The two of them worked the crowd from each end of the stage. The DJ mixed hits from T-Pain to Tank. Carmen hadn't lied when she said the stage set would be sexy. Scarlet took to the pole and began rolling up the pole to flip and drop into a split, while Carmen popped her ass and showed off her muscle control by moving one butt cheek up and down – right cheek, left cheek. Both Carmen and Scarlet gave each other the eye for a crowd teaser. Scarlet walked over to Carmen and undressed her. Money flew everywhere!

"Ahhh, shit, y'all, the show is starting now!" the DJ proclaimed over the microphone.

Carmen then handed Scarlet her whip and bent over. Scarlet smacked Carmen's ass with her left hand and whipped her with her right. Carmen made her ass clap and turned around to face Scarlet. Taking Scarlet's top off, Carmen pressed her face into Scarlet's breasts and began motorboating her. The girls gave a good show indeed. They ended with both of them on the pole in a 69 position.

"Ahhh, man, did y'all see that! They made it thunderstorm in here tonight! Carmen and Scarlet y'all," the DJ announced.

While getting their money swept off stage, Carmen said in a bubbly voice, "Scarlet, thanks. It was a success, and your pussy smells good too. Let's try another set together one day."

"Thank you, I guess," Scarlet replied with a confused face yet flattered by the comment.

Later that night, while driving home, I wondered about what Carmen had said. I'd never looked at a girl like that, and getting compliments from such a Goddess-like beauty as Carmen flushed my body. I weirdly smiled to myself as flashes of the night replayed in my mind. *I was really licking on her. I was tingling. Thank God we have to wear G-strings.*

***

The next night, Carmen and Scarlet did another stage set. That set was as successful as the one the night before, and to add a cherry on top, there was a man who wanted to get a VIP show from both of them.

"Carmen, I'm down, but I've never done a two-girl VIP before," Scarlet said nervously, although her insides were jittering with excitement at the thought.

"Oh, girl, it's easy. It's just like the stage but, of course, we're a lot closer. Would you feel comfortable with that?" Carmen asked.

"Well, that dude can't touch me, but if it's you, I don't mind. We're selling the fantasy," Scarlet said, but her thoughts were running wild. *Oh, I hope she touches me. I'm so turned on, and I don't know why.*

"Well, shit! Let's get this nigga for all he got," Carmen replied.

"Let's go!" Scarlet said, chuckling, and walked out to the main floor to get their customer.

"Hey, baby, you ready?" Carmen asked the man.

"Yeah! Yeah, I'm ready," said the man excitedly.

"Baby, we were thinking we could do it big for you," Scarlet mentioned.

"Alright, what y'all got for me then?" asked the man curiously. By the looks of it, the man was well off; he was wearing an expensive watch and a branded pair of shoes. Scarlet knew this from her chats with Jackson back in the day. He would always say, "You can tell a lot about a man from his watch and shoes."

Scarlet took the lead and said, "Well, baby, by the looks of things, you've had a hard day, and need to relax. Let's do the Champagne Room. It's about two hours with just us. Nobody else."

"Alright, so how much?" the man asked.

"Oh Scarlet, do you think he can afford it?" Carmen asked, poking at the man's ego.

"Oh yeah, he can. You got it, baby. It's $1,500 plus a $500 tip for each of us," Scarlet said.

The man's eyes went wide, but Scarlet grabbed his face and stared into his eyes. "You want us, right?" she asked while caressing his inner thigh and then rubbing her hands up to his shoulders and touching Carmen's waist. Scarlet had them in what looked like a group hug.

"Ahh, baby, you breaking me down," said the man in his country accent.

"But you got it, honey," Carmen said, pushing her chest up.

"Aw, hell, come on. Y'all bad!" the man said and began walking towards the VIP rooms.

Carmen and Scarlet shrugged at each other. They each grabbed one of the man's arms, standing on either side of him, and showered him with compliments to make him feel good about his decision. Comments like, "He's such a gentleman" and "He's got all the money."

When they arrived at the check-in for the Champagne Room, Scarlet took the lead and told the host what they were doing.

"Hey love! We're doing the Ace of Spades tonight," Scarlet said.

"Oh yeah! Right on, my man!" said the host giving the man a fist bump.

That was a boost of confidence for Scarlet, as she had only sold an Ace of Spades once in her Vegas club. See, the bottle was one of the most expensive items to be sold in the club, and hence, this made her feel very accomplished. She was on cloud nine.

"Well, baby, we have the room for about two hours, so we can chill, drink, dance, and drink some more," Carmen said in her bubbly voice.

Scarlet nodded. She knew they weren't going to do the whole two hours, so she kept an eye on the clock and not the monitor. Finally, the dance began, and the VIP waitress brought up the Ace of Spades bottle with some fruit.

"Y'all enjoy," she said, closing the curtains behind her.

"Thanks, we will," they all said in unison.

Carmen and Scarlet wasted no time dancing on the platform in the middle of the room. The room was a nice size and was decorated in Greek décor. This made a man feel like money. Marble figures mimicked the Athenian times, with a water feature on the wall. The room was dimly lit with a platform in the middle and an oversized white couch. There were some vine plants on columns in the corners of the room.

The man was happy and enjoyed his champagne, chats, and show. Scarlet and Carmen worked out that they'd dance for 10 minutes and chat with the man for 20 minutes. On their last show, Carmen suggested Scarlet dance for them.

"Scarlet, can you dance for us? I like watching you dance," Carmen pleaded.

"I suppose, but that means I need the last of the champagne," Scarlet said in a flirtatious manner.

As Scarlet got up to walk over to the platform, Carmen smacked Scarlet on the ass and cheered her on. "Ayyyeeeee, she so sexy!"

Since there wasn't a pole on the platform, Scarlet stood up and moved sensually to the music playing. Zoning out, she closed her eyes and began rolling her body down to a squatting position and popping her ass up and down. Carmen and the man clapped.

Scarlet smirked at them both and gestured for Carmen to come to her. Carmen got up and went to Scarlet. Scarlet was on her knees on the platform and reached for Carmen as she approached. Carmen smiled and leaned in to kiss Scarlet.

"Oh my God, yes! I didn't know this was going to happen. Yes, girls!" the man yelled out with glee.

Carmen and Scarlet paid the man no mind. Whispering to one another, "We got him," they continued to kiss. Carmen took control of the situation and began to kiss Scarlet on her neck down to her chest, then began sucking on her breasts. Scarlet was enjoying every moment. She forgot that she was doing a show.

Carmen slid her right hand down to the outer part of Scarlet's G-string and began moving her fingers back and forth. She could feel Scarlet getting more and more aroused. She came back up to see Scarlet's face and asked, "You like that?" and Scarlet replied, "Yes."

"After this, meet me in the showers," Carmen whispered, and Scarlet nodded. Getting her head back in the game, Scarlet smiled at the man and asked in a sassy voice, "So, did you enjoy your show, sir?"

"Oh yes! It was so worth it. You girls did well," exclaimed the man.

"Well, that's it, we're done," Carmen said.

"Alright, my card is with the cashier. I told her to hold it just in case."

"Aww, that was sweet baby. Well, tell you what, we can still do dances, but we need to go and refresh for you," Scarlet said eagerly, ready to finish the proposition with Carmen.

"Oh, okay, I can wait," the man said.

"Alright, we'll cash out for this session, and we can start a new tab for another one once we're back," Carmen said.

"That's a good idea, Carmen," Scarlet said.

As they walked to the cashier, Carmen conveyed to Scarlet that getting the money on a cash advance hit his pockets, not theirs, as the club took a percentage if they were to do "funny money," which was the club's credit card money from credit cards.

"Always make sure you have these niggas do a cash advance, so you get your cash upfront, hun. The club will take their percentage and the percentage from the dance, so you only wind up making half of your money," Carmen explained.

"Oh wow! Thanks, good to know," Scarlet replied.

Once the transaction was done, Scarlet and Carmen moved to the showers to refresh themselves for whatever else the night had in store for them. While in the shower, Carmen kissed Scarlet and told her to stay quiet. Scarlet nodded, and Carmen kissed her on her neck ever so gently and began sliding her hands down in between Scarlet's legs. Kissing her shoulders, Scarlet held on to Carmen and moaned lightly in her ear. Then, moving her hand in between Scarlet's leg, Carmen felt Scarlet's pussy pulse. Feeling overly excited, Carmen knelt and began eating Scarlet out. Scarlet was losing her mind, as she didn't know what to expect. This was her first time with a woman.

She closed her eyes and enjoyed the moment.

Later, when I thought about the encounter, I couldn't believe it'd happened. I'd never been with a woman before, and the experience left me in a daze. It was different from being with a man. Although the tingling sensation had nearly been the same, I felt more energized and flushed with a woman, like she knew exactly what could turn me on without me having to lead the way. I wondered if this would have ever taken place if Scarlet didn't exist.

Because now, Scarlet was Naomi. And I was Scarlet.

Chapter Fifteen

"Hi, Naomi, I'm Karla. I'll be your advisor throughout the process and completion of your college career," the college advisor said as she reached her hand out towards me.

After a long hiatus, I'd finally decided to return to school.

"Hi, Karla, it's nice to meet you. Thank you for taking the time to meet with me today," I said, shaking her hand.

"Of course. In chatting with you over the phone, you said you want to return to school and also change your major, correct?" Karla asked.

"Yes, I did traditional college, and it wasn't for me. I believe the University of Phoenix (UOPX) will be a good fit," I suggested.

"Right on. Let's get started. We'll go over your past transcript and see how many credits can transfer over. Then, we'll take a look at the business path and figure out what path will work best for you here at UOPX," Karla explained.

"Great! Also, I want to fast-track my path. I understand that is possible if the funds are available, correct?" I asked.

"Yes, that's correct. I see you read through my entire email and attachments. You're already off to a great start, Naomi!" Karla said, beaming at me.

I grinned and nodded my head in a silly manner.

"Let's begin, shall we?" Karla asked, walking me to her office for the registration process.

"Lead the way."

***

Two years had flown by, and I was still only working at the club, but I started to need something more. Although money and business were good, I couldn't fathom the risk of being Scarlet full-time. I needed a professional backup plan. I'd enjoyed my time out of school, but somehow my gut feeling told me it was time to go back.

In 2010, I registered at the University of Phoenix Las Vegas. I changed my major to business rather than education to benefit the profession I'd like to be in. Knowing the ins and outs of the front desk, I began chasing the goal of becoming the Vice President of Hotel Operations in a hotel in Las Vegas.

I knew how to run a business. Scarlet was a business, and I did very well with that, and I knew the workings of the front desk. Majoring in business just made sense. Attending the University of Phoenix Las Vegas was a nontraditional way of returning to school. The campus was not your typical college campus with dorms and yards; this campus was located inside a business center. I went to school twice a week in the evenings, which still gave me time to work and travel. I had a plan, and it was working.

***

"Hey, babe, what you got going tonight?" Daniel asked when he called up.

"Nothing. What's up?" I replied.

"I was thinking I'd take you somewhere special tonight. You've been so busy with school and work that I think you need a break," Daniel suggested.

"Oh, really now?" I replied with a bit of sass.

"Yeah. I'll pick you up at 6:30 p.m. Wear something fancy. We steppin' out tonight!" Daniel said exuberantly.

"Okay, babe, I can do that. Ouuuwww!"

"I love you," Daniel said.

"Love you too. See you soon," I replied.

Daniel had been living in Las Vegas for the last couple years. We had remained really good friends, but the more time we spent together, the more the lines got blurred. He knew I did not want a relationship, but it never stopped him from trying. Our love for one another developed into something magical. We knew we were one. We never discussed it in detail because our actions spoke for themselves.

Also, I never liked talking to Daniel about us because I knew I'd consistently break his heart every time he'd ask me to be his girlfriend. I knew I couldn't be with him fully because of my line of work. After Rodney, I never wanted to feel used or abused because of what I did. Daniel was different because he knew I was coming home to him, and he knew my business mind. He adored that about me. He adored me.

***

On July 16th, 2011, Daniel and I received news that he'd be deployed to Afghanistan. This put a hole in the both of us, as we were unsure as to when he'd return. The deployment was scheduled for nine months, but we knew better from his previous deployment.

"What do you want to do, Naomi?" Daniel asked.

"I don't know. We just started getting going and making plans. I'm scared, and it's different this time around because we've been face to face and practically living together. During your last deployment, you weren't living here yet, so it made it easier for me," I cried.

"I know, baby, I know," moaned Daniel as he reached out to embrace me.

Daniel began to kiss me and wipe away my tears. "We're going to get through this."

I nodded and kissed him back. He pushed his pelvis into mine, and we began kissing harder and more passionately. Daniel was a great lover, and he knew how to please me. Taking his right hand up the left side of my body, he tilted my head to the right and kissed my neck softly while using his other hand to pull me in closer.

As we stumbled over one another and made our way to the couch, he picked me up and began to kiss me from my mouth to my neck, to my stomach, and below my waist. Leading his tongue into my inner thighs and spreading my legs wider to get his head in between, he began eating me out. His tongue was golden. He knew I loved it when he ate me out.

Not allowing me to push him away, he asked, "Right there?" and I responded with a pleasurable, "Yes! Keep going. I'm about to cum!"

He continued until I came and kissed his way back up. His penis was ready, and I was ready to receive him. As he entered me, we both moaned, and our connection was sealed. Our bodies moved in rhythm with one another. Our spirits became one.

CHAPTER SIXTEEN

The business was raking it in, and all was well work-wise. I'd been dancing for five years now, and I was what they called a "seasoned dancer." Being a full-time exotic dancer and traveling, I'd seen a lot, but haters came a dime a dozen. A lot of dancers at most of the clubs hated when I came to work because they knew I was about my money, and I wasn't fucking with any of them. They talked trash but never stepped up until one night while I was in my Dallas club; this bitch tried it!

"Coming to the stage, ladies and gentlemen, all the way from Vegas, is our sensually, sinful Scarlet!" the DJ announced over the microphone.

Scarlet came out and performed her show like any other night. However, there were a lot of whispers and noise coming from one corner of the club. Coco's corner.

Coco was a local Dallas girl who worked in the same club as Scarlet and Zari, but Coco didn't like Zari, so she didn't like Scarlet. Coco stood 5'10" with heels on. She had an athletic body, and her skin was like whipped shea butter.

156

Coco and Zari had had a little misunderstanding at a house party they'd done together, and they seemed to have never gotten over it. Coco only worked at the club from time to time, but the times that she did, she was always causing drama for Zari and Scarlet.

"Oh, look who it is, little Sin City Princess!" Coco yelled out from the corner of the club, clapping extremely loud over the music and getting Scarlet's attention. Scarlet glanced over to see that it was Coco and blew her a kiss. This was Scarlet's silent way of killing her haters with kindness, which was another reason they hated her. She wasn't bothered by them. By anything.

Getting little attention from Scarlet, Coco fumed with anger and started yelling, "Go home, hoe! Go home, hoe!"

Scarlet threw her head back slyly and laughed in her direction as if Coco were cheering her on. Then, she continued with her stage set like nothing was wrong. Coco tightened her fists and continued to shout insults; however, it appeared as though with each insult Coco threw at Scarlet, the latter earned greater revenue. Scarlet was being showered with dollar bills.

Once Scarlet was finished, she quickly went to the dressing room to refresh. Shortly after Zari entered the bathroom, Coco came into the dressing room; a rectangular-shaped, narrow room with a long vanity in the middle. On each side of the vanity were gray lockers for each of the dancers. The bathroom was located in the middle, on the back wall facing the slit of the vanity, and the house mom sat opposite the bathroom. The room was centered around the well-lit vanity.

"So, both of them working tonight?" Coco spoke loudly to a few of her friends. She was standing at the end of the vanity near the house mom. Scarlet cut her eyes over to the right to see Coco, who turned her head towards Scarlet and smirked. "Yeah, I'm talking about you, hoe!" she yelled out.

With poise and glorious grace, Scarlet moved her neck just enough to survey Coco in one suave glance. And then, as though Coco had been sending chocolate kisses her way, Scarlet replied in a honey glazed voice, "Don't be mad because I make more money than you, honey. It's just how it is." Scarlet shrugged, her eyes smiling with victory.

"Fuck you and your cousin. She's never doing another party with me again!" Coco shouted.

"And that's fine. You do hood rat parties anyway," Scarlet replied, brushing her long, luxurious hair, and whipping it back to look at Coco.

Another dancer chimed in and clapped with every word she said. "Co - co, you're - a - hood - rat. Chill - out. You - ain't - on - their - level."

This dancer was cool with Scarlet and Zari and had traveled a bit with them to other cities and clubs.

"Haaaaa!" Scarlet taunted, high-fiving the other dancer.

"Bitch! Come see me outside." Coco's face was blood red as she threw lipstick towards Scarlet, who ducked in time for the lipstick to crash against the vanity instead.

Scarlet was taken aback. She was used to jarring comments once in a while, especially from Coco, but a physical attack was beyond her imagination.

How could she tolerate that? Her eyes glared with fury as she rose to her full height again and felt conscious of all the other girls' stares on her.

No, I am not gonna lie back.

Scarlet's mind pranced like a fox. She took off her heels and began pushing through some girls who were standing between her and Coco. Coco scoffed and twirled her hair on her finger. Scarlet gritted her teeth and banged one of her heels on the vanity to get the girls moving.

Coco continued to talk shit. "Ah, bitch, come and get me."

"Oh, I'll get you," Scarlet screamed at the top of her voice, and the girls jumped up.

Coco grinned, raised her hand, and waved a middle finger to Scarlet, who was already riled up enough not to care.

"Bet, bitch! Let's go!" Scarlet bellowed and threw her mirrored heel at the astounded Coco.

The heel swiped Coco's head, and Scarlet jumped over a couple girls' dancer bags. She was furious and tried her best to get to Coco.

In the heat of the argument, Zari came running out of the bathroom and yelled, "Let's go, cuzzo! I heard that bitch."

Coco moved quickly behind the house mom's area. Hearing the commotion, the manager came into the dressing room, and Scarlet yelled, "You betta get her before I do. Scary ass bitch!"

"Coco," the manager shouted, raising his voice above the existing commotion, "in my office, now!"

Walking away, he turned back and said, "Scarlet, I'll be with you in a moment. Please stay in the dressing room."

"Yeah, go handle her because I don't need this shit," Scarlet replied.

Zari went over to Scarlet and asked, "What happened?"

Still fired up, Scarlet looked at Zari and laughed. "That bitch is a hater. Fuck her! Want a snack? I got noodles."

Scarlet found her cool returning to her. Naomi was asleep, and Scarlet had done what was necessary. Phew! She blew strands of her hair off her lips.

Zari looked puzzled and replied, "Sure, I'll eat with you."

They ate while Scarlet waited to chat with the manager. He soon came out asking for Scarlet.

"Scarlet, I'm ready," he gestured, nodding his head for Scarlet to come to his office.

"Alright, here I come," Scarlet replied.

"So, what happened, Scarlet? I've never seen you so upset before," the manager probed.

"It started while I was on the stage. Coco kept yelling out disrespectful stuff, and that wasn't cool. I remained calm because of our customers. But, when we got into the dressing room, she provoked me by talking loud, calling me names, and throwing her lipstick at me," Scarlet explained, using her scholar's voice.

"I heard about that from the DJ. That wasn't cool," the manager agreed.

"Exactly. Like, who does that?" Scarlet said with attitude, shrugging and rolling her right hand up into a flat palm.

"Well, we like you here, and I know you pay a lot of money to be here, so I've handled the situation. Coco will no longer be able to work the nights you're here. I've moved her to days," said the manager, sounding anxious for Scarlet's approval.

"Yes, I do pay a lot to be here, and I make the club a lot of money while I am here. I appreciate you taking the lead and handling Coco because I was 'bout to beat her ass!" Scarlet said.

"We don't want that," sighed the manager, nervously chuckling with relief.

Scarlet knew she was an asset to the club because she always tipped everyone out. Tipping everyone that mattered. Tipping showed Scarlet's status and that she made money. Everyone loved money!

Chapter Seventeen

Daniel had been gone for almost three months. He left at the end of August, and I was still working like crazy. I was using a lot of my money to pay for school. Paying to fast track my degree had its advantages. One advantage was finishing early, but the tuition was much more. I used my own money and student loans to pay the fee.

While journaling for a class, it dawned on me that I hadn't had my period in what seemed like months. I couldn't remember when my last period was, and my period app had reset itself, not saving any of my logs.

Naomi, are you pregnant again? I can't be. I feel like I am. Oh God, what if I am? I've been drinking a lot at work. Oh no, Lord, help me. What will Daniel think? Do I really want this baby? I can't have a baby right now. How the fuck am I pregnant? I've been taking birth control. Oh shit! I've been fucking up on my birth control. Surely it's still working – or is it? Damn! I gotta go to the store after this journal entry.

All these negative thoughts swarmed my head, but I repositioned myself quickly into survival mode.

Don't panic, girl; you can handle this. I heard Scarlet's voice. *First things first, get five pregnancy tests and piss on all the sticks. Tell no one!*

***

"Hi, honey. Looks like you need to know, huh?" the cashier at Walgreens commented as she scanned my Clear Blue, First Response, Walgreens, and Clear Blue Digital pregnancy tests across her scanner. The cashier was an old white lady named Peggy with white hair. She beamed at me; her smile as bright as the gold-framed glasses she wore.

"Yeah, I gotta know. Have to be sure." I returned her smile politely.

"Well, good luck, love," Peggy called out as I left the store.

Little did she know, I wasn't going to go through with the pregnancy. I had way too much on my plate, and Daniel was gone. *What would I look like bringing a baby into this chaos?*

Daniel and I weren't even together. Hell, we didn't know what we were.

***

Test 1. Clear Blue pregnancy test: Plus sign...*Pregnant*

Test 2. First Response pregnancy test: Two lines...*Pregnant!*

Test 3. Walgreens pregnancy kit: Two lines...*Pregnant!!*

Shit!

Test 4. Clear Blue Digital: *Pregnant!!!*

Test 5. Walgreens pregnancy kit: Error; lines weren't clear

Four out of five? We're *PREGNANT!!!!*

***

"Hello, I'd like to make an appointment for an abortion," I said, calling the abortion clinic.

Considering the secrecy of my plan, I did at first contemplate looking for a new abortion clinic that didn't have my records, but then, I wondered, would it be worth it to go through all that hassle? And I already was quite satisfied with the service I received last time. Plus, it had been some years since my last abortion, so I was hoping they didn't pull my file. And if nothing worked, I'd learned not to care.

"Sure, do you know that you're pregnant? When was your last period?" the receptionist on the phone asked in a kind, sweet voice.

"Honestly, I have no clue. I think it was about three months ago," I replied confidently.

"All right, honey, we have an opening this week on Friday, November 4th at 8:30 a.m. Will that work for you?" asked the receptionist.

"Yes, that's perfect!" I yelped.

"Have you been here before?" she asked.

Swallowing deeply, I took a deep breath and said, "Yes, ma'am, unfortunately."

"Oh, it's no problem; this just makes it easier for the paperwork. Can I get your name?" she asked.

"Naomi, Naomi Bowers."

"Give me a second while I go get your file. I need to confirm your date of birth and emergency contact. One moment please," she urged.

While waiting on hold, I thought, *Wow, I'm doing this again, but for some reason, I don't feel as bad. I don't feel anything. Is it because I'm not as far along as before, or am I really that focused on my career? Hmm.*

"All right, Naomi dear, can you give me your birth date and emergency contact?" the receptionist asked, picking up the call again.

"Sure. My birthday is November 26th, 1987, and my emergency contact is Susan Bowers, 702-717-0899."

"I got you all set, hun. See you Friday. Please do not eat or drink anything after 8 p.m. Thursday. On Friday morning, this means do not have anything – no water, coffee, or even brushing your teeth. We need to make sure the body is fully cleansed."

"Got it. See y'all on Friday. Goodbye."

After getting off the phone with the clinic, I had to contact Daniel. We hadn't spoken in weeks, and email seemed to be our best line of communication when it came to talking about serious stuff.

Email

> November 2, 2011, at 2:32 p.m.
>
> Hey baby,
>
> I hope all is going well for you in Afghanistan. All is well here in Las Vegas. I can't complain. It's been a while since we spoke, as the phone cut us off a couple weeks ago. I hope you are safe, baby. I miss you a lot. I received some news today, and I have made a decision.
>
> I'm pregnant. However, I'm not going to keep the baby. I'm unsure how far along I am, but we did get it in a lot before you left, so I'm guessing maybe three months or two and a half months. Not sure. I hate that I had to tell you this in an email, but this seems to be our best form of communication. I decided not to go through with the pregnancy because one, I'm in school, and two, you aren't here, and we haven't established a solid foundation of what we are and what we're doing. I do hope you understand, and hopefully, if you're feeling up to it, we can chat or email about it. Until then, take care, love.

I love you.

-Your Ms. Bowers xoxo

Send.

Friday came, and still no word from Daniel. I wondered if he had even seen the email. It felt weird knowing that he'd probably find out once everything was done, and he wouldn't get to discuss it with me. I didn't need a discussion, as I always believed my body was my body and I could do what I wanted with it; my body, my rules. Perhaps this was different from the last time: I didn't feel as guilty as back then. I didn't feel scared like I originally had. I didn't cry myself to sleep or worry myself to death. I wasn't a pregnant high school girl who was shit scared about her image. I'd become the daring woman with enough money in her wallet and wisdom in her mind to harness her decisions.

***

Mom drove me to the clinic, and the car was quiet until she said, "Naomi, you sure, baby? I can help you if you change your mind."

"OMG, Mom, nah, I'm good. I have plans for my life, and having a baby right now will set me back. Also, Daniel and I don't know what we're doing. I want to be married and have a stable foundation for my child. I'm not as stable as I'd like to be." I smiled at my mom, devoid of any feelings to mask.

"That's smart, baby. Well, I'm just saying it would be nice to be a grandma someday. I ain't getting any younger, ya know." Mom chuckled and raised an eyebrow.

"Yeah, yeah, yeah. Thanks, Mom, for driving me and taking care of me today. This procedure shouldn't be long, nor should the healing take long either," I said.

Unlike last time, I didn't feel jitters when thinking of my condition. In fact, I was quite impatient to get done with the procedure.

"It's okay. You know, you're always welcome at home. I like you home. Shoots, you ain't married; you should come home. You know, in the olden days, girls had to stay home until they were married," Mom began battering on.

"Mommmm!" I yelled.

She rubbed my head. "Okay, baby. Mommy just loves you and misses her baby, that's all."

"I love you too, Mom," I replied, grabbing her hand and holding it.

The clinic still looked the same. We drove down the private drive and approached the all-white building. Parking the car, Mom got out, and I followed. She ran over to hug me and whispered in my ear, "You are strong, and you are beautiful. I got you."

"Thanks, Mom. I needed that," I replied.

We walked up to the clinic. The sliding glass doors looked so sleek and shiny, just like before, and as we walked through them, I felt a sensation of déjà vu. There was no turning back now.

"Good morning!" the receptionist said at the front desk.

"Morning. Naomi Bowers for 8:30 a.m.," I said, signing in at the desk.

"Perfect, Ms. Bowers. Do you have a driver here with you today? If not, you'll be in recovery a bit longer. Your procedure shouldn't take long, but if you're driving yourself, love, we have to wait for all the anesthesia to wear off before sending you home," the receptionist stressed.

"Oh, wow, I didn't know I could drive myself, but I brought my driver today," I said with a sarcastic half-laugh. *Who the fuck would want to drive themselves home after an abortion? Shit!*

"Great. And what's your driver's name? We'll need to call him or her when it's time for them to pull around to pick you up," the receptionist said, all bubbly and giddy.

"It's my mom. Her name is Susan. Mom, come over here," I said, calling my mom over to the desk.

"Oh, perfect, thank you. Hi, mom, I just needed to see your face, so I know who I'm calling when Naomi is done." The receptionist smiled.

"Just call for Naomi's mom. I'll be here," Mom replied, hiding her nervousness behind a calm expression.

"All right, Naomi, once the nurses find out how many weeks you are, they'll let you know how much your procedure will cost today. From your phone call, you think you're three months, so that's about $750. But they'll let you know because anything less than 11 weeks and 6 days is $500," the receptionist explained.

I didn't care how much it cost. I had $1,000 cash on me for the procedure.

I replied, "Money isn't an issue." I grinned sheepishly at the receptionist.

"Oh, ah… that's great," she said. "You and your mom can go take a seat in the lobby. The nurse will call you when they are ready for you."

We went and took a seat. Mom sat nervously next to me and kept rubbing my left leg and repeating, "God watch over my baby."

"I'll be fine, Mom," I told her casually, squeezing her palm.

"Naomi!" the nurse from the back called out.

Mom stood up with me, and I hugged her. "Imma be fine, Mom. See ya soon. Read a magazine," I suggested while walking to the back.

"Hi, Naomi, I'm your nurse, Lisa. I'll be assisting your doctor today with your procedure," she said, guiding me to an exam room and gesturing for me to take a seat next to the examination table.

Unlike my previous one, this examination room looked like my OB/GYN's exam room. It was light and airy, and there wasn't any music playing.

"I'll need to take your vitals and have you pee in this cup. I'll also need a small blood sample, so I'll be using this small needle to prick your finger and this super small tube to collect your blood." She showed me her medical instruments.

"Okay," I replied, easing into a chair. I was very relaxed and ready to get it over with. "Lisa, will this tell you how far along I am?" I questioned.

"Yes. Once we know how far along you are, we'll be able to settle the payment for your procedure today."

"Perfect!" I replied. "Let's get started."

Once the result came back, Lisa said, "Naomi, looks like you're not as far along as you thought. According to your results, you're about 11 weeks."

"Oh, cool. Wow, I haven't had a period for that long," I said, amazed.

"Yeah, if you're a busy woman, sometimes you can lose track of your periods," Lisa explained.

"So, I owe $500 for my procedure today?" I asked.

"Yes, your total including pain meds, if needed, is $500. You can go pay at the receptionist desk, and I'll go get the doctor. See you in a bit."

"Sounds like a plan to me," I replied. I got up and took my payment to the receptionist's desk. I made sure to stay behind the door, as I didn't want to panic my mom. She was so nervous.

After the transaction, when I went back into the exam room, the doctor walked in behind me. He was an old man with a polite smile. "Hello, Naomi, how are you doing this morning?"

"I'm good, doctor, and you?" I replied.

"Well, well. Thank you for asking. I'm Doctor Hall, and I'll be performing your procedure today. It'll be quick. I'll sedate you with a local anesthetic and clean out your womb. The total time of the procedure with recovery, so the anesthetic can wear off, will be three hours. Do you understand?"

"I understand."

"Do you have any questions for me, Naomi?" he asked.

"Yes. What is the total recovery time? How long do I need to be off from work?" I asked.

"Given that your procedure isn't too extensive, you should be able to return to normal activity in about a week or so. I'd recommend no heavy lifting for three to four weeks," Dr. Hall said.

"Got it."

"Also, you'll need to come back for your post-op appointment in a month. The receptionist will give the time and date to your mom."

"Please make the appointment for the morning. Anything after noon is not good for me," I said.

"All right, I'll have Lisa let them know at the desk," the doctor said. "Well, let's get started, shall we?" He walked out, and Nurse Lisa walked back in.

After her came Dr. Hall and his team, which was a nun and the anesthesiologist. I recognized him to be the same guy who had sedated me before, Dr. Neil. He didn't seem to have recognized me, but if he did, he did not make it obvious. The nun didn't surprise me this time around.

"Naomi, will you be fine with Sister Marie being here? She will be here to pray us through this procedure," Dr. Hall said.

"Yeah, that's fine. Prayer is good," I replied, beaming widely at the nurse, who seemed slightly amused at my courage.

"You're a brave woman, Miss," she said, and I smiled.

"And Naomi, this is Dr. Neil. He'll be our anesthesiologist today for the procedure," Dr. Hall said.

"Oh yes, I know him." I grinned at Dr. Neil. Recognition dawned upon his face, and color rose to his cheeks.

"Oh, I'm sorry, but of course I remember you," he said – a little embarrassed, I guess, for pretending not to remember me – and then he added, "Umm... I didn't think you were comfortable knowing that I...um...remembered you?"

"It's all right," I said.

He smiled politely.

"Okay, let's begin," Dr. Hall said.

As I got positioned on the examination table, Dr. Neil stepped forward and placed a clamp on my middle right finger. "This is to track your pulse and blood pressure, dear," he said softly.

I nodded.

"Naomi, I need you to move down on the table. You want to feel like your bottom is going to fall off the table," Dr. Hall said, motioning with his hands for me to move down. I wiggled down, and he said, "That's it, perfect."

As before, he was very gentle and explained everything he was doing. I listened to Dr. Neil's voice and took a few relaxing breaths. Before I knew it, I was out.

***

"Naomi, dear. Wake up. You did well." Dr. Neil's voice woke me up in the same way he had done previously.

My body shivered and fluttered.

Oh goodness, this feeling again.

"That's the anesthesia wearing off. You're fine. These warm blankets will help," Dr. Neil explained.

Nurse Lisa came over and smiled. "Naomi, you did well. I need you to hold on to me."

"Bathroom, huh?" I said, fading in and out, trying to look up at Nurse Lisa.

"Yes, you have to use the bathroom if you want to go home now," she replied.

I nodded, and using all my strength and holding on to Nurse Lisa, I stumbled over to the bathroom and plopped down on the toilet, realizing I didn't have my panties on, but rather a diaper with Velcro sides that Nurse Lisa undid for me.

"Thank you," I said weakly, and Nurse Lisa rubbed my back, helping me to stay conscious. After what seemed like a lifetime, drops of urine hit the toilet basin. Once I was done, I tried to get up but fell back down, and Nurse Lisa held on to me tightly.

"Whoa, Naomi, not too fast, hun. I got you. Let's put your panties on." She helped me fasten the Velcro and then walked me to a back door, where my mom had the car pulled up. Nurse Lisa helped me get into the car's front seat. "Naomi, you're safe and with your mom now. Call us if you have any questions," she said before closing the door slowly.

***

Email

November 22, 2011, at 9:40 a.m.

Hey Ms. Bowers,

It's been crazy here, and I haven't had much time to contact you. I'm safe, though. Reading your email was a stab to my heart. I'm so sorry I wasn't there, baby. I was happy and sad all in one emotion. You know I'd love for us to have a baby. I'd take care of you and my baby. I wish we spoke more about our future, damn. I miss you, and I hope you're well. I'll try calling you soon. I love you, my sexy teacher. I know, I know, you've changed majors, but you'll always be my Ms. Bowers. Muah xoxo

-Your Danny Bear

November 22, 2011 at 1:11 p.m.

Hey Danny Bear,

I'm happy to hear you're safe. I don't want to go back and forth in an email about everything that's taken place. Just know I'm fine and well. I miss you! Chat soon. I'll be waiting for your call. xoxo

-Naomi

Send.

***

Months passed. Daniel and I spoke and agreed to discuss us when he returned in May, but as time drew nearer, we drifted apart. When he got back in May of 2012, he was very closed off. He didn't talk much about his deployment nor us. Sleeping together was not the same. Our sex was not the same. We were not the same.

"Danny Bear, what's wrong? We're barely talking, and I don't feel we're connecting anymore," I said.

"Baby, I'm fine. I've been busy with work, and you know my hours have been long. I feel bad that we can't spend time like before," Daniel explained.

"I know, but that's why I've been working less, trying to make time for you, for us. You sure there isn't anything you want to get off your chest?" I asked, looking him directly in his eyes.

They were black. No emotions. I'd heard stories of military men going away for deployment and coming back a different person. I hoped this wasn't the case for my Danny Bear.

"Naomi, leave it alone. I'm good. We good!" Daniel said, raising his voice and walking away.

"Damn, that got serious fast. Don't walk away from me! And don't yell at me either. I was just asking," I yelled as he turned around to face me from across the room.

"Alright, fine. I'm still sad about your abortion. It's been eating me up since I found out, but while away, I did something that has followed me home."

My heart dropped. "Like what?"

"I slept with another woman, and she's also stationed here in Vegas. I see her every day, and we both act like nothing happened, but coming home to you just kills me inside," Daniel said, walking over to me.

I froze. My heart sank to the bottomless depths of my soul, and my eyes dried out as if they were shedding invisible tears. Minutes ticked by, and I stared at him with an open mouth. His expression shifted from irritated to guilty real quick.

"So, let me get this right," I said, my voice all crass and choppy. "You were mad or *sad*...." I stressed the word for extra effect, "about my abortion, and so you decided to go fuck another woman?" I raised my hands in the air.

"Well...I am sorry, Naomi," he said. "It just happened. You know I love you. And, well, it wasn't as if we had made an official commitment of 'us' back then...."

He knew it the moment he said it. His face went white as he heard his own words. A painful smirk gashed across my face. He opened his mouth again to apologize or justify, but no words came out. I breathed heavily, staring at his ashen features.

"I didn't mean that…" he blurted out.

Grief exploded inside me.

"Oh, I get it now," I said spitefully, forcing my tears back. "It's my fault, isn't it? It's my fault because I always kept you on your toes. Because I thought we couldn't be together due to my line of work. Because I never wanted to be the reason we lost each other. But you know what, where I really fucked up is when I thought we didn't need any validation or 'making it official' kind of thing because we were connected by our 'souls' or something. Because I thought our mutual love was enough. Oh, how wrong was I!"

I melted into emotions.

"No, no, no…" he reached out, pulling me close, but I jerked away from his arms.

"It's cool, Daniel. We were never together anyways. I'm out," I said, wiping away the few teardrops on my face. Within minutes, I grabbed my things and began to walk towards the front door.

"Naomi, wait! Nomi, baby! Don't say that. It's not like that. I was lonely and sad. I fucked up," Daniel cried out, running after me and positioning himself to block the door.

"It's good, Daniel, we weren't together. I'm leaving. I'm done. I thought we were better than that. We used to tell each other everything, the good, the bad, and the ugly, but instead, you held back from me and pushed me away. I'm done. Ugh. Move," I said, pushing him out of the way so I could leave.

"Naomi!" Daniel yelled.

I kept walking and never looked back.

Although we hadn't officially defined our relationship, I felt a pain like never before. He'd hurt me to the core. I genuinely and truly loved that man. Driving home, I wondered, *Was it my fault he went off with another chick? Were we together? And had I only said we weren't to cut him, so he could feel my pain? I'm glad I didn't have his baby. Nigga would have had me fucked up coming home to a pregnant girlfriend and he done fucked the next bitch. Thank you, God, for helping me dodge that bullet. But I still love him. Damn! I'm going to be alright. I gotta stay focused. I can do this. To hell with him.*

The tears began to fall.

Chapter Eighteen

"Dear parents, friends, and loved ones, we'd like to welcome you to the University of Phoenix Las Vegas Commencement Ceremony of 2013. Let's give our graduates a round of applause for their excellent efforts. You did it!" the announcer exclaimed gleefully.

The crowd roared with excitement as they all cheered for their loved ones receiving their degree.

"Naomi!" My family shouted, cheered, and flashed their homemade signs with my name on them – "Naomi, you did It!" "Go Girl!" "Talk Only Business to Me – Naomi."

I looked up at their section and blew kisses to all of them.

I did it! I really did it. Thanks, God!

Feeling overjoyed and accomplished, I began making plans to get out of the club and transition into the corporate world. I put in applications everywhere from the Marriott to the MGM Resorts. I planned to work my way up and take any leadership position they had open once I paid my dues.

Las Vegas hotels care little about your degree; they care about seniority. I learned that in an interview at a Marriott hotel. They wanted
to start me off at a base salary of $14.60 an hour. I happily declined, as
I had experienced being a front desk agent at the Hilton some years
ago, and although I'd been making $13.80 an hour, I now had an edu-
cation under my belt. I figured that would count for something.

"Thank you for the opportunity. The wage is too low given my previous experience and degree," I said to the hotel manager who was
interviewing me.

"I agree, Naomi. However, times are changing. We want people
with degrees, but experience takes precedent over degrees," the hotel
manager explained.

"Wow, good to know. Thank you again for the opportunity," I
replied, pushing my chair in to leave the office.

During my job hunt, I continued to work at the club. That being
my only source of income, I had to make a schedule and begin tracking
my money to learn my hourly wage and if all the time I was spending
in the club was worth it. I always kept a journal of my nightly earnings
and deductions, but tracking the hours spent in the club with an hourly
rate was something new. I figured by doing this, I could get a realistic
view of how much I could settle for when going back to the corporate
world.

Night 1:
Check-in at 10:30 p.m. and off at 4 a.m. (Slow fucking night!)
Money made: $500
$500 divided by 5.5 hours = $90.90 an hour

Night 2:
Check-in at 10:30 p.m. and off at 4 a.m. (Better)
Money made: $913
$913 divided by 5.5 hours = $166 an hour

Night 3:
Check-in at 10:30 p.m. and off at 4 a.m. (Okay night)
Money made: $707
$707 divided by 5.5 hours = $128.54 an hour

Night 4:
Check-in at 10:30 p.m. and off at 4 a.m. (Shit night)
Money made: $339
$339 divided by 5.5 hours = $61.63 an hour

Night 5:
Check-in at 10:30 p.m. and off at 4 a.m. (Great night)
Money made: $1,031
$1,031 divided by 5.5 hours = $187.45 an hour

I tracked my hours and spending every time I went into the club to work. Most nights were great, but shit nights were shitty. I found that once I got back into the hotels, my average hourly rate could be no lower than $16.90 an hour. This hourly rate would take care of all my bills. I wouldn't be able to travel as much, but my necessities would be taken care of.

I had a plan, and I decided to stick to it. I continued to apply for front desk positions around the Valley and work at the club until one day, I got an interview at an independent hotel on the Las Vegas Strip. It was a small boutique hotel, but the HR lady interviewing me was an old friend's mom. I hadn't seen her since her daughter, and I danced in high school.

"Naomi Bowers! I thought that was you when your application came across my desk," the woman said happily and embraced me with a hug.

"Hi, Ms. Holmes, how you been?" I replied, hugging her back.

"Good, and you? You know, my daughter is a mess. I'm a grandma now. I gotta tell her I saw you," she replied.

"Oh wow. Nene always said she didn't want any kids. That's a surprise, but good for her. But I'm good. I graduated not long ago and been trying to get back into the hotels to build my career," I mentioned.

"I see. Good for you! I wish Nene was on it, but God has other plans for her," she said and stared into space for a brief moment before continuing. "Well, looking over your application, it seems you definitely tick all the boxes, but the position is part-time, and the pay is $15 an hour. Your insurance will kick in once you complete 300 hours. We're non-union, too. At the Hilton, were you union?"

I nodded, taking in all the information, and replied, "Yes, at the Hilton, I was Teamsters. I know I have to start somewhere, but I do need a hotel that is union, as I have my pension there, and I'm almost vested."

"I understand, honey. You got to do what's best for you," Ms. Holmes said, smiling and nodding her head.

"Thank you for the opportunity, though, Ms. Holmes. I've been going on interviews right and left, and all of them have been saying they'll call me back, but no word yet. This interview gave me hope." I chuckled with relief.

"Aww, honey, it's tough out there and very competitive. Keep your head up and keep pushing along. God will make a way for you," Ms. Holmes encouraged me.

"True," I replied.

"Naomi, I wasn't sure if this would be appropriate, but something has dropped in my spirit, and the interview is over. Will you come and visit my church?" Ms. Holmes asked shyly with her hands clasped together near her face.

I was taken aback by this sudden request and didn't know how to react.

"Oh, Ms. Holmes, I don't know. It's been a minute since I've been to church," I said hesitantly.

"It's okay, honey, God wants to see you," she said with a smile.

As she said those words, I felt goosebumps on my body. I took a deep breath before responding.

"Umm... alright. Do you know how to text?" I asked.

"Yes, I do, honey!" Ms. Holmes said, picking up her phone and shaking it.

"Cool, just text me the time and place. I'll come," I said with a shaky voice.

I didn't know why, but suddenly, I had this strong urge to cry. Something came over me, and I resisted the tears hard. All I could do was tell Ms. Holmes that I'd come.

Without a minute's hesitation, Ms. Holmes texted me her church's information: "Naomi, service is this Sunday at 11 a.m. The address is 713 D St. New Church Fellowship. I hope to see you there (smiley face)."

I texted her back: "Thanks, I'll see you Sunday."

Driving home from my interview, I thought about the conversation again.

God wants to see you, she'd said. But he sees me every day, I thought. What am I going to wear? Oh goodness, what am I getting myself into?

Well, my grandma always said, "Come as you are," and so I'll go as I am, but appropriate. Don't want to piss off the church people or God.

I continued my week as usual – the club, home, and interviews. Lately, I'd started feeling like a robot. Saturday night came, and I went to work but stayed only until 1 a.m., as I knew I had an early start on Sunday with going to the church and all. It had been years since I'd stepped foot into a church.

As a young girl, I used to go to church with my grandma before she passed and then with my great aunt, but once I got old enough to stop being at my aunt's house, I stopped going. Mom didn't force me either. As a child, she was forced to go to church and do everything in the church, which in some way, she built up some resentment towards the church when she got older, and they judged her for her career. This also showed when a couple of my grandma's church friends came to her wake and judged Mom again for not dressing in what they felt was appropriate attire for a funeral.

"Umm, Susan, what are you wearing?" one of the old church ladies had asked Mom in her southern, old lady voice.

"A dress, ma'am," Mom replied.

"Oh. It's a little tight, ain't it?" the lady asked.

"No, it's just fine. It's a simple black dress. Do you need a plate or want me to make you something, ma'am? I don't have time for this," Mom replied.

"Nah, I am fine, baby, but you know if your mama stayed at our church, she would've lived a longer, more prosperous life," the lady said with a tight-lipped smile.

I remember Mom's expression. She stared at this lady as though she'd slap her if she wasn't at the funeral.

Mom replied, "We made the right choice moving churches, and since you feel that way, you can leave. Get out of my mama's house. God don't like ugly."

The lady had grabbed her things and left. That memory stayed with me. From then on, the Baptist church was not my church. I believed in God and Jesus, but churches, ugh! I had zero time for church, especially once I got old enough to voice my opinion.

***

Sunday morning had come, and I got up and got myself ready.

Ms. Holmes texted me: "Naomi, you still coming today, honey?"

I texted back: "Yes, ma'am. See you soon."

Although I was going to church, I still wanted to be fashionable. I put on a pair of black slacks and a white blouse with ruffled sleeves that buttoned up the middle. I threw on a pair of black Christian Louboutins, and out the door, I went.

The drive to her church seemed to take longer than expected. I was so nervous driving there. I maintained the speed limit the entire way and drove with no music on. My thoughts were getting the best of me. *What if I walk in and lightning hits me? Oh goodness, what if someone recognizes me from the club? Nahhh, that can't happen. They probably all holy and sanctified.*

Pulling up to the church, I parked in the nearby parking lot and walked over to New Church Fellowship. The church was small. It looked like a white box with tiny specks of green grass surrounding it. The steps leading into the church were wide and had chipped paint peeling from them. The doors were white and opened wide in the middle, leading the way to the sanctuary. The long, dark brown pews sat one behind the other, creating two columns and ten rows facing the altar.

As I walked in, Ms. Holmes was looking back and spotted me. She came and greeted me with a big hug. "I'm so happy you came!" she said.

"Aww, of course. Thanks for inviting me," I replied.

Praise and worship began, and I recognized one of the songs, "He's Able." The church's band had an awesome guitar, drum, and piano player. The singers weren't your traditional choir. There were only five of them that stood and led the songs. Their voices pierced through my soul with an abundance of pure joy I'd never experienced before. I found myself swaying to the songs and lip-syncing to a few of them I recognized from a distant past. The last song had me in tears.

"That's the spirit of God moving through you, honey. Feel it. Let God in," Ms. Holmes whispered in my ear, handing me a tissue. My tears dried, and I listened to the sermon.

The preacher was a dark-skinned young man who didn't dress like a preacher. He wore a pair of blue slacks with a button-up collared shirt tucked in. He looked like he was about to go to a business meeting. He spoke about the difference between being conformed and transformed. He read out of the book of Acts.

I didn't have a physical Bible, but I had downloaded the You Version Bible some years back to get daily verses. I used that to read along. To my surprise, many people had their phones or tablets out. Church had changed since I last attended. I liked that I understood the sermon. The pastor wasn't reading out of what could have been a newspaper. He read the Word and made real-life connections to it. During altar call, he called for people who wanted to be transformed by God's grace, and the praise and worship team came back on stage and began singing hymns and harmonizing. People fled to the altar for prayer.

Ms. Holmes grabbed me and gestured towards the altar. I shook my head frantically. She persisted, yet I gave a bashful look. She nodded and went ahead to the altar.

Before the altar call was up, a lady from the altar came down and began touching people.

Lord, please don't let her come over here.

God must NOT have heard me because that lady came straight over to me.

Oh God, I thought.

As I was still sitting down, she came over to me, looked me in my eyes, and began praying over me. She closed her eyes, so I closed my eyes and bowed my head. Her hands touched me, one on my forehead and the other on my back.

A strange, divine feeling flooded my soul. An unexplainable feeling. All worries, ideas, pains, thoughts – every little piece of thought in my mind was driven away in an instant. My eyes turned moist, and I began to cry out, lifting my arms high. "Lord, help me! I'm sorry! Thank you for keeping me safe, God!"

The lady continued in a language I'd never heard before. The pastor then walked up to me, and the lady praying for me slowly moved back and continued to pray, but in a whisper, while rocking back and forth.

I looked up at the pastor with tears still clouding my view. Relief and compassion leveled through my bones, and I relaxed. *I am safe.*

The pastor had a blank expression but calm eyes. When he spoke, his voice felt as though it were coming from far away, yet so close that it could have been in my mind. He said, "You're new here. Welcome. God has told me to tell you that He loves you, and He hasn't left your side. You're going to be teaching nations. Trust HIM."

I nodded, and he left without another word. I had no clue what'd just happened, and I sat there in a daze. The pastor walked back to his podium and calmed the church. I was still in awe of what I'd experienced. It was mysterious, yet familiar. External, yet very much intimate. It was as though I'd received confirmation of something I didn't even know I needed confirmation of. I expected the church service to last for three hours, but it lasted for an hour and a half. I was happy about that. It was too much at one go, yet I wished I could go back in as I walked out of the doors.

Once we were out, I had questions.

"Ms. Holmes, thank you again for inviting me. The sermon was good. I'm happy I could understand it," I said with a chuckle.

Ms. Holmes laughed, "Girl, I know. Thanks for coming. This was the first time in a long time that the pastor came down from the altar to prophesize. I knew God had something planned for you!"

"Huh, prophesize? What does that mean?" I asked.

"Pastor is a prophet of God. He's able to hear God and use His words to speak to people like you. Pastor prophesized to you today. God used Pastor today to talk to you. God used me to get you here," Ms. Holmes explained and began jumping in place. "See, you getting me excited. Let me stop," she continued with a joyful laugh.

"Oh. I think I get it. Do you know why that lady started praying for me in a different language? I have never heard such a language," I exclaimed.

"Oh, baby, it has been a while for you." Ms. Holmes laughed and continued to educate me. "She was speaking in tongues. That's her spiritual language," she explained.

I nodded with a confused face. "Oh, okay. It has been a while. Well, thank you again, Ms. Holmes, for inviting me. Tell Nene hey."

"Of course, honey. You come back whenever, okay?" Ms. Holmes said as we parted ways to walk to our cars.

CHAPTER NINETEEN

Email

Dear Naomi,

We are happy to inform you that you have been chosen to join our team. Your New Hire Orientation begins on November 11, 2013, at 9:00 a.m. Please be advised that orientation is a week-long process. We hope to see you soon. Have a great day!

Yours Truly,

MGM Resorts

"Woohooooo!" I yelled, dancing in place after reading the email.

I have a week.

I made a plan to work all week and pay up my rent for three months just in case my schedule took a moment to become steady. When I'd applied for the front desk position for MGM Resorts, they didn't specify if the job would be full-time or part-time.

In the interview, they said, "It will be determined, as we have many candidates to hire."

I was fine with that because they were Teamsters Union. I only needed to get vested, so I could begin working my way up the ranks.

What did that pastor mean? Teaching nations? That pastor has no clue. I want to be Vice President of Hotel Operations one day.

I hadn't been back to Ms. Holmes' church, but the pastor's words rang loudly in my head every day. I tried making sense of it all, but I couldn't figure it out. I continued my days like every other day: work at the club, come home, go to interviews, and check my emails.

***

On the day of orientation, I wore a pair of gray slacks with a black long-sleeved button-up, slim fit for women, and pulled my hair back into a ballerina bun, baby hairs swooping out and in on each side of my forehead. I paired it with black Aldo loafers. Your girl was cute! I was ready.

Driving to orientation, I said a quick prayer:

Dear God, please be with me through this process. Allow me to learn quickly. Thank you again for always being here with me. Amen.

Pulling up to the MGM Resorts parking garage, I had to check in as an employee.

"Hi, I'm Naomi Bowers. I'm here for the New Hire Orientation," I said to the security guard.

"Welcome to the team, Naomi!" the guard said. "Here's your temporary parking placard. Make sure you keep it in your window at all times, whenever you come to work."

"Oh wow, cool. Thanks for the info," I replied and pulled off to find a parking spot.

When I finally made it into the boardroom, it opened to about 130 people. I was not expecting this! *What in the world? Why are so many people here?*

"Hello. I'll need your name, sweetie, so I can check you in," a kind woman with an iPad said.

I told her my name and answered a few more questions. She gave me a printed label of my name and department and asked me to have a seat.

Walking into the boardroom, I held my head high, beaming proudly at everyone who caught my eye. Many people smiled at me.

What a great day!

The room smelled of coffee and fresh air. I found a seat at a table with one Black IT guy, a Mexican IT guy, and two white women, one from housekeeping and the other a host for one of the restaurants. They looked like a pretty down-to-earth group. They were laughing and appeared happy. This attracted me to their table. Plus, they seemed to belong to my age group.

"Hello, everyone, I'm Naomi. Front desk," I said, waving to them and taking a seat. Soon, I'd made acquaintances with all of them. *Happy people, happy work life!*

***

During my orientation, I met my trainer and supervisor. She was a short, young Malaysian woman.

"Hi, Naomi, I'm Tina. I'll be your trainer for the next couple weeks. On the desk, I'll be your supervisor, so if you face any issues, just call me over."

"Hi, Tina, nice to meet you, and thanks," I replied. "Is it just us? I see other trainers with groups of people."

"Yup, it's just us! This is awesome because we'll have the front desk training room to ourselves, and we'll be able to break and start as much as we want," Tina replied enthusiastically.

Perfect! Exactly what I wanted. A personal trainer. Could the day get any better?

I followed Tina out of the boardroom, down a long concrete hallway.

The hallway led into the casino, and Tina began a tour, leading me to the front desk. "Hey, y'all, say hi to Naomi. She's new!" she said as we walked past. Everyone at the desk waved, and their guests checking in waved too.

"So, Naomi, this will be your usual route each day you come to work. You'll bypass the boardroom and report to me here, at the front desk in this back office," she explained. "If you get lost, just call me. I'll come to get you."

"That's a lonnnng walk from the garage to here," I said, chuckling.

"Yes, it is! But you'll get used to it. All of us have," Tina replied, laughing.

I felt a sense of freedom in my new workplace. It was very different from the club. People here smiled at one another for no reason. In the club, that would mean "business," but here, it meant hospitality. Powerful positive energy surged through me as the day went by.

After we left the small back office, Tina led me to the training room. It looked like a college auditorium lecture room with a mock front desk and computers. Tina explained the working of the software and systems I needed to be acquainted with, and I followed her lessons carefully with jubilant attention.

The training lasted for two weeks, well after my birthday. By the time I made it to the desk, I was 26. I didn't have a set schedule, as I was the "new girl" and lowest on the seniority board. My schedule went from swing shift to graveyard to mornings. My sleep was all out of whack.

Given my blotchy schedule, I still worked at the club. If I worked at MGM Resorts during the morning shift and had the next day off, I went into the club that evening after I was off the desk. If I worked swing or graveyard, I usually had two days off to reset, so I'd work at the club one of those nights that I'd be off.

At the hotel, I was happy with my work. At the club, I was pleased with the money. But something tiny, yet significant kept nagging at me in the back of my mind. Whether at home, work, or the club, I couldn't forget what the pastor had said: *You're going to be teaching nations. Trust HIM.*

Chapter Twenty

The Calling

By January 2014, my schedule had gotten a bit more predictable. I worked the 3 p.m. to 11 p.m. shift three days out of one week, and the following week I'd be on graveyard doing the 11 p.m. to 7 a.m. shift for two nights. My check usually only had five days on it, and I got paid biweekly. It was tough, but it was consistent, and I liked that. Given that my shifts were more consistent, it became easier to go into the club and make some extra money every month.

***

"Coming to the stage, we have our sexy Scarlet," the DJ announced.

With each beat, Scarlet walked down the runway, as usual, swaying her hips from right to left and looking at each man sitting around her stage. She grabbed the pole, reached her right hand up, and walked around the shiny brass pole, showcasing her body and long legs. She then grabbed the pole with her left hand, lifted her body, and wrapped

191

it around the pole, swirling down like a snake onto the stage floor. Crawling on the floor and stopping to pop her black G-string, she collected her money.

Scarlet did her routine, but the night was slow. She didn't feel enthusiastic like she normally did. When she'd walked into the club that evening, her body hadn't felt right. Something was out of order. She thought it might be because of Naomi's shift from the previous night. But once her stage set was done, she couldn't help thinking about what the pastor had told Naomi. *You're going to be teaching nations. Trust HIM.*

Being in the club, she felt bad for thinking of church. She shook the thought and continued to work.

The club had three customers, and none of them wanted a dance from any of the girls in the club. Scarlet tried her luck, but still, nothing.

You're going to be teaching nations. Trust HIM.

She thought to herself, *God, what is going on? I need to make at least $300 tonight. It's pushing 1 a.m. and still no money in this bitch. Ugh!*

She walked to the dressing room to refresh herself and get her head back in the game. When Scarlet returned to the main floor, there was only one customer left, and he was sitting at the bar.

"Hey honey, want some company? You're all alone up here." Scarlet spoke to the man in the sexiest voice she could muster. Her confidence level was low on the inside, but she faked it quite nicely.

"Hey hun. Nah, I'm good. I'm just gonna finish this beer and get out of here," the man replied.

"Alright, well…" Scarlet sighed and stood up, but in the midst of her dialogue to woo the man, she heard a voice. A deep, resounding voice. Every other sound in the room appeared to have muted itself, and this new voice boomed over everything with crystal clarity.

It said, "NO. LEAVE."

Scarlet took a step back, her eyes widening into ovals.

"Umm… did you say anything?" she asked the man, who looked at her casually.

"Ah… yeah, I just told you that I was going to drink my beer and get out of here."

"No, I don't mean that… Something else. Did you say anything else?" Scarlet asked.

He shook his head, perplexed.

I must have been hallucinating. Oh God, Scarlet thought. *Well, I need to get this man, though.*

So, she again opened her mouth to convince the man. But again, the deep, serious voice resounded in her ears.

"*NO,*" it said. "*LEAVE.*"

She blinked and made a third attempt at the conversation, and yet again, "NO. LEAVE."

The man at the bar got up, staring at Scarlet as if she was weird, and waved a hand in front of her face. "You okay?"

Scarlet stood frozen to the spot, the imprint of the voice fresh on her ears.

"Um… I'm fine," she said, and the man relaxed.

"Well, you look tired, hun. Perhaps you should rest a while." He'd said something that no man in the club had ever told Scarlet. And to her astonishment, she believed him.

"Have a good night," he said before walking away. Scarlet waved him off, still intrigued.

When she looked around the club, it was empty. Scarlet walked around the emptiness and sat down in an armchair. All of a sudden, everything went silent. No music, no clutter, no chatter, no nothing.

Scarlet breathed lightly, feeling conscious of her space. And then she heard it again.

The voice. This time, it was louder, clearer, and held an ominous power.

"*LEAVE,*" it said. "*IT IS TIME TO GO.*"

Scarlet shivered and wrapped her arms around herself. *I just need to make $300, and then I'm out.* But the voice, the power, was clear in its instruction.

"*NAOMI. GET YOUR THINGS AND LEAVE,*" it said as she shivered a bit more, "*AND NEVER RETURN HERE AGAIN. THIS IS IT. LEAVE NOW.*"

Scarlet felt goosebumps rise on her body. She looked around. There were no customers around, only a few staff who were busy with their work. None of them seemed to have heard any voice. Or anything, really.

Feeling frightened, she wondered, *Am I tripping? Am I hearing shit?*

"*NOW.*"

Scarlet stood up immediately, her heart throbbing faster.

"*NOW!*"

She ran to the back to the dressing room and cleared her locker out. She threw everything away except her bag. The voice rang louder and louder in her ears.

It kept repeating, "*GET YOUR THINGS AND LEAVE AND NEVER RETURN HERE AGAIN,*" blocking out all of Scarlet's what-if thoughts.

She moved quickly and left the club. As soon as she made it into her car, all she could do was cry out, "God, why!"

Tears were streaming down her face in a sudden reflection of her experience. The voice seemed to be with her throughout. And then, slowly, her "whys" turned into "thank yous." As she cried, she heard the voice again, one final time.

"*TRUST ME*," he said.

***

After the experience in the club, I never went back and continued to work at the MGM Resorts. I managed to bid on a shift. I was now working graveyard, but I noticed that my health began to decline rather quickly whenever I had to go in for work. My body ached, and I couldn't get my allergies under control. I went to the doctor to make sure I was okay, but when I went, he said, "Everything looks normal, Naomi. It could be a light case of anxiety."

"Huh, anxiety? No," I replied.

"Anxiety comes in many forms. Do you feel better when you aren't at work?" the doctor asked.

"Yeah, I feel great, actually," I answered.

"But when you get to work, your body begins to shut down, right?" he probed.

"Correct. It's like I get sick," I replied.

"Yeah, sounds like something could be triggering this subconsciously," the doctor replied.

"Hmm, never thought about that," I said.

"Yeah, it can happen sometimes throughout life. I suggest taking some time off to figure out what makes you happy and see if you can bring that happiness to work with you," the doctor suggested. "In the meantime, take it easy and get lots of rest. You'll be good."

"Thanks, doctor, for the suggestions. I'll be sure to do so," I replied.

On the drive home from the doctor's office, I noticed there were many billboard signs advertising for substitute teachers needed in the Clark County School District (CCSD). On the radio, too, the same ads were playing. That evening while watching TV, I kept seeing commercials for CCSD needing subs. "Come be a CCSD substitute! Teach tomorrow's future!" they'd say. My interest was piqued, but I was over education a long time ago. Feeling confused, I did the only thing that I hoped would work.

I prayed.

Dear God, You said I should trust You, and I'm doing that, but I don't know what's going on with me. It's been months now since I left the club, and work isn't all that great either. I need Your guidance. Help me. What am I supposed to do? I know I want to be in the hotels, but this CCSD thing is looking pretty good. Help me, Lord. I'm struggling. Amen.

I guess God heard my prayers and had different plans because the MGM Resorts cut my hours. I went from working graveyard to on-call. I couldn't catch a break. Feeling down and out, I texted Ms. Holmes: "Hey, Ms. Holmes, can I visit your church again?"

Send.

In less than a minute, Ms. Holmes replied: "Yes! Yes, please come! (smiley face)."

I was lost, and nothing was going my way. I felt confused and utterly perplexed about what I wanted in my life, what I was already doing, and what plans God might have for me. Nothing seemed to work to fix it. My problem seemed bigger than me, and I had no one to turn to. The doctors couldn't fix this feeling. My parents and friends couldn't fix it either. It was a tugging feeling, and the only time it seemed to go away was when I was praying. I began praying all day, every day. I spoke to God about everything.

Sunday came, and I was eager to go to church. It looked the same, and though it had been a while since my first visit, many people still recognized me. They welcomed me with hugs and handshakes, saying, "Welcome back!"

I felt a sense of belonging. My mind was clear; I didn't have any worries in the world. The pastor's sermon was on point. I felt like it was made for me. He discussed temptation and how you won't know who you are unless you go through things. God allows us to take tests so we can know that we can make it. We come out better after the test. We read out of the book of Matthew. I marked it all up so I could go back and read the entire book. The verses spoke to me, and the pastor's sermon made sense to me.

During the altar call, I made the sound decision of giving my life to Christ.

April 5th, 2014, my life changed. God came in and made a way for me. He turned my current situation upside-down. I wound up quitting the MGM Resorts the following day and applying for the substitute position with CCSD. God made it all possible! He guided my steps. The process was so easy.

Although I was fearful, I kept hearing Him say, *"TRUST ME."*

I trusted him.

By April 15th, 2014, and by the grace of God, my substitute license was approved, my interview with CCSD was done, and I landed a contract with a middle school I was familiar with. Talk about listening to God and following His way! I was done fighting and bargaining with God.

Thank God for directing my path to obtain my business degree; it was all for this moment right here! See, I got the contract at the middle school because of my degree, despite only having a week's worth of experience as a substitute teacher.

The school district was trying a new Science, Technology, Engineering and Mathematics (STEM) program, and they needed people with solid math and business backgrounds. I didn't think I would qualify, but I got the position. I kept hearing God say, "*TRUST ME*," and I continued to trust Him; however, I did feel upset when I couldn't afford my own place anymore.

Thoughts swarmed into my head. *Girl, you can go back to the club and just make some money real quick. God is working too slow right now.*

I tried returning to the club to dance, but all the expenses related to the club made it challenging. I had to buy new shoes and outfits because I hadn't danced in a while, and the house fees had increased. Everyone at the club knew I'd left to be holy and live a "normal" life.

"Coming to the stage is our Sexy Saint Scarlet," the DJ announced repeatedly for a couple months.

Scarlet walked down the lit runway night in and night out, trying to make money, to make ends meet, until one night something was different. She didn't have that sway in her walk, nor did she look happy.

Why the fuck am I even here? She wondered in misery. *How in the world did God let me come back here? Ugh!*

Scarlet continued her stage show, but she pranced around on stage until suddenly she stopped. It was as if she'd frozen.

The DJ saw Scarlet frozen and tried talking over the mic to buy time for her to snap out of it.

"Alright y'all, let's see some more money on this stage. Scarlet ain't gonna move until she sees some money," he announced.

But Scarlet was stuck.

If only I could move right now. I would leave. This shit is for the birds. I ain't making any money, and I'm barely breaking even on my outfits and house fees. Fuck this!

The DJ announced the final song on Scarlet's set, and Scarlet regained her movement. She snapped out of the trance, and then, immediately, she walked off the stage. There were boos and jarring comments by some customers and other strippers. Scarlet drowned in humiliation while she walked back to the dressing room.

And for the first time in her life, Scarlet cried. She looked at her arms, her legs, and every part of her body she could touch and feel, and she cried. She wept inconsolably.

After a while, she breathed heavily and rubbed away her tears. She stood in front of the mirror and stared at herself. But she couldn't see herself in there. Behind the ruined, half-washed-off makeup, the woman who looked back at Scarlet wasn't Scarlet.

"Naomi," she whispered.

And Naomi smiled through the mirror at Scarlet.

"Naomi." Scarlet repeated the name.

An intense warmth flushed through Scarlet's body as she stared at Naomi, who didn't have any struggles of money, desire, or stress. The confident, grown, and happy woman – Naomi.

It was as if she had an epiphany about what she was to become. In that moment, Scarlet left the club yet again, never to return. Naomi, on the other hand, had already begun the path laid out for her by God.

***

With all the changes in my life happening so rapidly, I didn't have enough money to make ends meet. My savings had been drained by previous rent and bills. My head was barely above water. I didn't know how to go home. I felt like a failure. I didn't understand why God would do this to me. He'd given me everything I had thus far, but I didn't have enough to live on my own. At 26, I moved home.

"Dad, can I chat with you?" I said when I visited him.

My voice shook, filled with embarrassment, and I asked, "Dad, can I live with you? I would ask Mom, but her place doesn't have room."

I began to cry.

"Aww, baby, of course! It's about time you came to your senses and came home. Daddy would love for you to live here. You get to be around your brothers. They're going to love having their big sister around, and I know Patricia would love to have another woman in the house to chat with," Dad comforted me and continued with a slight chuckle, "I don't think Wine Wednesdays will be the same anymore. You won't have to drive home. This will be your home, baby."

He kissed me on the cheek and yelled for Patricia and my younger brothers to come downstairs.

"Everyone, Naomi is coming home!" he said happily.

"Woohoo!" one of my younger brothers shouted.

"So, you want to share my room with me, Nomi?" my other little brother asked in an innocent voice.

Stopping me before I could answer him, Patricia said, "My baby is coming home. I'm the luckiest stepmother ever. I'm so proud of you!"

She leaned in to embrace me and kissed me on my cheek while I broke down into tears, leaning on the kitchen island.

Answering my younger brothers' questions, Dad said, "Naomi is getting her own room. Maybe you can ask her if you can sleep with her once she gets settled in."

They jumped up and down with excitement.

Dad grinned, "Y'all go upstairs. Daddy and Mommy gotta talk to Nomi real quick."

"Okay," they said in unison and ran away.

"Why are you crying, baby? This is a happy moment," Dad said, concerned.

"Dad, I feel like a failure. I have been on my own since I was 19. Paying my bills and getting myself through school too. Why is all this happening now? I'm dang near 30!" I cried out.

"Aww, there's nothing to be embarrassed about, love. We all need help from time to time," my stepmom said, still embracing me. "You're doing the right thing by coming home and not putting yourself into debt."

I took a deep breath in and exhaled. "You're right. Thank y'all. I love you guys."

Dad walked over to the kitchen island and pulled Patricia and me into a tight hug.

"Group hug," he said, chuckling and continuing in a rhythm, "My baby's coming home, my baby's coming home! Daddy loves you!"

CHAPTER TWENTY-ONE

A few months had passed, and I was settling in well back home. My subbing job was going well until one day the principal and the head of the math department visited me during one of my classes.

"Ms. Bowers, your teaching and modeling is great. You keep your students engaged and involved," the principal said excitedly, looking like she wanted to say more.

"Thanks. Those workshops came in handy," I replied.

"Aren't they great? I enjoy going to the workshops myself," the head of the math department agreed.

"Well, Ms. Bowers, there've been some cutbacks, and they are cutting the STEM program here next year; however, we want to keep you as a math teacher. We also like that you've started a jazz dance team, and we don't want to lose that either. None of us are trained dancers," the principal explained.

"Oh, that's sad to hear, but I'm flattered you all want me to stay. Being a sub has its ups and downs. Getting this contract with the school has been great. I've enjoyed working with my team and the dancers," I replied.

"I understand. I started off as a sub too," the head of the math department stated.

"There's only one thing, though," the principal said and continued hesitantly. "For us to keep you and for you to renew your contract here, you'd have to show that you're forwarding your education. Workshops and professional development don't count. You'd need to go back to school to get your master's in education and get fully licensed as a teacher."

"Oh wow! I never thought about returning to school. Umm, can I get back to you? I'll need to do some research on master's programs around the Valley." I was taken aback.

"Well, Ms. Bowers, we've done some of the legwork for you. We know how organized you are and how you like getting all the facts before making a decision, so we contacted the district and asked who they'd recommend for teachers to get their licensure from, and they said National," the head of the math department rambled.

I nodded, trying to take it all in, and then I remembered the voice. "*TRUST ME.*"

"All right, I'll look into it," I said confidently.

"Yayy! We will support you throughout the entire process, Ms. Bowers," the principal said, smiling and looking relieved.

***

I liked the school I was at, and they worked with me. They allowed me to share my ideas freely without any judgement and, they didn't treat me like a substitute teacher. I was a part of the team. They also allowed me to help with their dance department, which had been nonexistent until competition time or when funding was needed. When the opportunity presented itself to work with a young group of students who wanted to dance, I took the responsibility of coaching and molding them into a fantastic jazz team. Though God had pulled me from the exotic side of dance, He still blessed me with the gift of dance, and I was grateful He didn't take my gift.

By my 27th birthday, I was enrolled in the master's program at National University. This program was all online and offered me my master's in education and my Nevada licensure.

2014 was the year of change for me. I accelerated my program by taking two courses a month rather than the typical one class every five weeks. I did not want to go back to school, but I knew God had a plan for me. I stopped doing things my way and followed God's way. His way was a lot easier.

***

One Sunday, while I was at church, things began to make sense as to why God had moved me home. The sermon was about saying goodbye to old situations. Leaving all of what I knew and had accumulated from my dancing days was an old situation. It was clear that I couldn't bring that money, that lifestyle, or my tainted memories with me on my new journey. I had to say goodbye to it all without pretending.

I felt a feeling on the inside of me, similar to the feeling I had on my first visit to New Church Fellowship. My eyes were filled with tears, and all I could say was, "Thank you, Lord."

After the service, I spoke with the pastor and asked him some questions.

"Thank you for the good word today, pastor. I do have some questions, though," I said.

"All right, Naomi, let's go into my office and talk for a bit," he replied.

"Sure," I said, following him to his office. Taking a seat, I began, "So, sometimes during prayer and even during a sermon, I get this feeling that is like a fluttery, joyous feeling. It's as if I can't control it. I burst out into tears, and I just can't stop thinking or saying, 'Thank you, Lord.' Does that feeling have a name?" I asked him.

Nodding, the pastor responded with a smile, "Oh, Naomi, that's the Holy Spirit coming over you. We all have a spirit that lets us know when God is present."

"But I don't get up shouting or kicking my shoes off or running around the church like other people when the spirit hits them. So, is it different for everyone?" I asked.

Chuckling, he replied, "The spirit hits people differently, Naomi. God speaks to us all differently, too."

"Got it. And my last question is, how do I know when it is God who is leading me and not my own will?" I questioned.

"Whoa, now that's a good question, Naomi. We know when God is leading us when we sit still and listen. You ever been praying, and you just stop and have a feeling of knowing what to do? That's God. Being still sometimes allows us to hear God more clearly, but if you are struggling to hear God, pray that He makes His voice clearer to you. You must also be willing to listen, too, Naomi," the pastor said with a firm voice, looking across his desk at me.

"Yeah, I've experienced that before. That makes sense. Thank you, pastor, for your time. I'll work on being still and listening more," I replied.

While driving home, the sermon's message resonated with my spirit. I accepted my new situation and thanked God for moving me ahead. As days progressed, God slowly revealed His plan for me and why He did what He did for me. He allowed me to go astray to bring me back to Him and mold me into His image.

When I thought I wasn't good enough for God's favor, He accepted me with open arms. God catapulted me into my calling, teaching, in less than two and half years. By the age of 29, I had received my master's in education and full licensure as a teacher, with two years of counted teaching experience under my belt. What takes people years to do, God did for me in two.

Was it hard? Yes, but He made it possible. In the words of Marvin Sapp, "I never would have made it, I never could have made it without you. I would have lost it all, but now I see how you were there for me. I can say, I'm stronger, I'm wiser, I'm better, much better. When I look back over all you brought me through, I see that you were the one I held on to, and I never would have made it without you."

I was now living in my purpose.

CHAPTER TWENTY-TWO

After receiving my master's and license in teaching, I came across the opportunity to teach abroad. The school I was teaching at had a sister school in Thailand that needed a single math teacher.

"Exciting news, Ms. Bowers!" the principal said, walking into my classroom after my 5th period algebra class.

"Really? What is it?" I asked curiously.

"Our school has the opportunity to send one of our very own over to Thailand," the principal exclaimed.

"Oh," I said, confused. "What school? I didn't know we had ties to schools in Thailand," I continued. Still very confused, I listened.

"Yes, we have a sister school in Thailand. It's an international school, so the curriculum is similar to here. But the most exciting part of this news is we feel you'd be the best candidate for the position," she yelped.

"Huh, why?" I asked.

"They need a single, young math teacher with bright ideas, and that's you!" she explained.

"Oh wow! So, no one else came to mind?" I asked. "Don't get me wrong, I'm flattered, but I need more information. I've never traveled abroad before. I mean, I've been to Puerto Rico, but that's American soil," I said, starting to get a bit excited and nervous.

"I can understand your concerns, but it's the opportunity of a lifetime. You can teach and travel the world, girl!" the principal urged.

"Yeah, yeah, yeah. Get me all the information first, and I'll let you know something in the next couple weeks," I replied.

"I'll do you one better. Let me know your final decision by the beginning of next month, and we can move forward from there." She clapped her hands and made a funny face.

"I will do that," I replied as we walked down to the teachers' lounge.

The principal kept her word and sent over all the information about the school that was in need. I read through all the material, and it was a pretty good gig. It was a two-year contract with annual bonuses, and if I decided to stay, there would be another signing bonus for that new contract.

The school was located in Phuket (Poo-Ket), Thailand. Phuket has sandy white beaches and is an island off of the mainland country of Thailand. The school days were the same as my current school, Monday to Friday, 8 a.m. to 3:30 p.m., with local national holidays, Christmas and spring break off. The salary was $20,000 more a year than what I was currently making. My current salary was $32,000 a year before taxes.

The extra 20K was making the opportunity in Thailand sound more enticing. The school had a population of students from all over the world, and class sizes were much smaller than at my current school. This was intriguing because I'd have fewer distractions in the classroom, and we could do more hands-on math projects. Although the opportunity was great, I was scared. I didn't know anything else than the United States of America. In my fear, all I could do was pray. I needed guidance, and though it was an exciting opportunity, I didn't want the money to cloud my judgement.

Dear God, thank you for all you have done for me and what you're going to be doing. I need your help. I am faced with what sounds like a great opportunity, but I'm scared. I don't know what to do. It sounds like this could be my way out of the States and a way to travel like I've always desired to do – but is this it? Do I take the opportunity? Shoots, I don't even know if I qualify like that. Lord, I ask that You show me the way and make Your signs and voice clear to me. I thank You in advance. In Jesus's name, amen.

After my prayer, I sat in my room in silence. I didn't discuss the opportunity with my family, as I did not want to get them excited or sad about any possibility that I would leave to teach abroad. With that, the weeks went by, and I didn't say anything to my principal about the position until one day, the school in Thailand reached out to me via email.

Greetings Ms. Naomi Bowers,

I am Cindy Moore from Phuket American International School. Mrs. Tims, your principal, has referred you as one of the candidates to represent your school here in Thailand. She sent us your qualifications, and you are just who we need. You have bright ideas, and you enjoy leading extracurricular activities for your school. I'd like to set a time and date for us to have a chat on Skype. Consider this your interview. You can ask all the questions you'd like. I do look forward to your response. Thank you and chat soon. Have a wonderful day!

Yours in education,

Mrs. Moore

Oh wow! I thought. *I didn't even put in my application yet.*

A voice sounded loudly in my head: "*TRUST ME.*"

Feeling confident, I replied to the email, and Mrs. Moore was delighted to hear from me. We set up a time and date to chat and began the process of planning for the next school year. Once I got the position in Thailand, I told my family, and all of them were happy for me, yet sad that I was moving away.

"So, baby, you gonna come back every holiday, right?" Dad urged.

"Yes, Dad," I said with a long, dramatic sigh and a smile.

Dad was the most worried, as he had all the questions. Mom and Patricia were excited and hoped I would get to travel more and meet someone.

"You're going to be living in paradise, love!" Patricia said excitedly.

"Hopefully, you find yourself a husband, too. We're not getting any younger over here. Grandkids would be awesome," Mom said.

Rolling my eyes, I replied, "OMG, guys, chill. It'll be a new experience for sure, but it is still work for me."

"Yeah, and all work, no play leads to a disaster." Mom laughed. "You're going to be fine. Although you're going for work, you still need to live."

"Yeah, you're right, Mom. Thanks," I said, pulling her into a hug.

CHAPTER TWENTY-THREE

Touching down on Thai soil in July of 2017, the song "Never Would Have Made It" by Marvin Sapp popped into my head, again: "I never would have made it, I never could have made it without you. I would have lost it all, but now I see how you were there for me. I can say, I'm stronger, I'm wiser, I'm better, much better. When I look back over all you brought me through, I see that you were the one I held on to, and I never would have made it without you."

The new school year had arrived, and I was grateful. Phuket was different from all my imaginations. The beautiful island offered bountiful scenery of beaches, green jungles, lovely sunsets, and great food. The people were kind and spoke some English. For those who couldn't speak English, I used Google Translate to communicate with them in Lao or their local dialect. I adjusted well to my surroundings.

I had a Thai partner who took me around to show me the sights my first week in Phuket and helped me find a place to live. I lived near the school, which was awesome because I could walk. In Las Vegas, I'd had to drive for hours to get somewhere. I'd told myself when I moved, I'd have a bike for transportation and walk more. So, that's what I did. In moving to Thailand, I felt sad that I was leaving home but happy that God had blessed me with the opportunity.

I taught children from all walks of life. They were from South America, North America, Africa, Europe, Asia, and also Thailand. I learned about their different cultures and how they lived, and they learned about mine. They were surprised to find out that despite being Black, I was also Filipino. They had never seen anyone of my race before.

"Ms. Bowers, are you Thai? Your skin is dark like mine," one of my students said.

"No, I'm Black, but I am also Filipino too," I replied.

"Oh wow! That's cool. So, your parents are Black and Filipino?" the student asked with a confused look on his face.

"Yes. My mother is mixed with both Black and Filipino; her father was Filipino. And my father is Black American," I explained.

"Oh, that's just like Nikki. Her mom is white, and her dad is Thai," another student yelled out, pointing at her friend, Nikki.

"Yes, exactly," I exclaimed. "Do we have any more questions before we get started? We can continue our introductions during the rest of this week. However, we need to begin with our content."

All the students in the classroom shook their heads and began focusing on the lesson.

The school year went on, and just like at my old school in Vegas, I started a jazz dance team and had performances to show off their skills every new semester. The school was excited to have a dance team, and having a trained coach was an added advantage because that was less money out of their pockets. The school would put on big productions for their community every semester to showcase a grade's learning or for the holidays before a major break. My dance team would perform in all of them. Watching them dance filled my heart with joy.

I would think, *If only they knew the half of it. God is good.*

***

In Phuket, there were many religions, and many of the church services were not in English. I had to learn and rely on my relationship with God. I watched online sermons from my old church when I could stream them. The internet service wasn't that great in my area, but I made do.

Learning about my relationship with God took time and effort. I read my Bible more and prayed and meditated on His Word. There were days that I felt like giving up, but God would speak to me and say, "*Trust me. You will be all right, for I am the truth, and I will not forsake you, my child.*"

Those words of wisdom and listening to gospel songs such as "Reflections" by Jason Champion or "I Smile" by Kirk Franklin helped get me through those tough times. Living abroad has its pros, but its cons can be daunting at times if you don't have a relationship with God.

I relied on praise and worship songs to get me through when I wanted to go home or needed to be filled with joy. God isolated me to mold me for what was to come. He taught me to rely on Him and not my judgement. As time went on, God allowed me to travel and see the world. I was able to visit countries that I had only read about in my history books or brochures.

Within the two years that I was in Thailand, I visited and took extended vacations to Italy, Greece, Germany, Indonesia, China, Spain, the Netherlands, Cambodia, and the United Kingdom. All of this was made possible by God. I thought that while teaching abroad, my salary would be minimal given that I'd want to go home for the holidays, but God increased my salary more than I could imagine. I used to think I was making money dancing in the club; that had nothing on this!

When I worked in the club, I couldn't travel out of the country, let alone stay for extended amounts of time to enjoy a vacation. God positioned me for greatness! When the time came for me to re-sign for another year at Phuket American International School, the Head of HR offered me more money, a bigger bonus, and a per diem position. This position was being a consultant for the school. I'd represent the school at different conferences and leadership workshops to market the school and bring in more business. I would be paid hourly during these times, and all my travel expenses would be paid for, too. God made this possible. And here, I would be able to use both of my degrees.

At the signing of my new contract, I heard a deep voice say, "*Well done, my child. But I'm not done yet.*"

***

Today, I am a living testament to God's mercy and love. He forgave me and showed me I was destined to do extraordinary things. I have taught the nations, and I currently consult for international schools around the world. God has done a lot more than having me teach nations. He is allowing people to see the God in me and learn from me. I am much more than I could have imagined!

I am Naomi Bowers, and this is my testimony on how I transitioned from stripper to saint.

A Message from the Author

Having the call to write, I wrote this book to give hope to young girls and women who look like me and women worldwide. I've added some of my own life experiences to foster a sense of reality in the book. Readers, this book is a testament to the fact that all women are great, regardless of their background and life experiences. No matter what we have encountered, God can still shape and mold us into the image He finds fitting for us.

Meet the Author

Davina E. Brown is an International Educator and currently resides in Xiamen, China. She was born in Stockton, California, and raised in Las Vegas, Nevada. As the eldest sibling out of three children, Davina has made it her duty to always set a good example for those around her – hence her robust educational background. Over the last decade, Davina has shared her knowledge and passion for education and the arts with students worldwide. She enjoys spending time with her family and friends and traveling the world. From Stripper to Saint is her first novel.